IRON TOWN BOY

Anne Ahmad

D1514438

PONT BOOKS

First Impression—2004

ISBN 1 84323 337 1

© Anne Ahmad

Anne Ahmad has asserted her right under the
Copyright, Designs and Patents Act, 1988,
to be identified as Author of this Work.

All rights reserved. No part of this book may be reproduced,
stored in a retrieval system, or transmitted in any form or by
any means, electronic, electrostatic, magnetic tape,
mechanical, photocopying, recording or otherwise without
permission in writing from the publishers,
Pont Books, Gomer Press, Llandysul, Ceredigion.

This book is published with the financial support of the
Welsh Books Council.

WORCESTERSHIRE COUNTY COUNCIL	
1 6 4	
BfS	30 Sep 2004
	£ 4.99

Printed in Wales at
Gomer Press, Llandysul, Ceredigion

For my father,
Evan Owen Thomas,
who first told me about Richard Trevithick.

Acknowledgements

For their kindness in reading and commenting on parts of the text my thanks are due to Sylvia Crawshay and Kingsley Richards. They are also due to Robert Protheroe Jones of the National, Maritime and Industrial Museum; Glyn Bowen; Philip Lloyd; Dorothy Craig; Geraint James; Caroline Jacobs and Richard Hicks of Merthyr Tydfil Central Library. The medieval Welsh poem quoted on page 26 was translated by D. M. Lloyd.

1

Gwilym's feet hurt. How long he'd been walking he did not know. Hours, it seemed like. His empty stomach was telling him so.

The Drovers' Way he was following stretched ahead: wide, well-trodden and empty of any other human being. A breeze stirred the prickly gorse bushes that bordered the grass-grown track and ruffled his own tousled hair.

Gwilym squinted up to look at the silvery winter sun and tried to tell the time. It was low on the horizon and somewhere on his right. It wasn't mid-morning yet. He had promised himself a bite of food half-way through the morning. He shifted the pack on his shoulder and went on.

He hadn't reckoned on his feet hurting so much. It was the big toe on his left foot that was most sore. If only he had a horse to ride, like Squire Jenkins' mare. He wouldn't have sore feet if he had a horse.

He loved horses. The exciting sound of their shod hooves clattering over cobblestones. He loved the flying manes and tails of them, their bright eyes, snorts and whinnies, the gloss and power of them. He'd love to work with horses. His mind full of them, he walked another mile.

A large smooth stone among a tumble of rocks fringing the wayside looked comfortable enough to rest on. Gwilym limped over to it and sat down, putting his pack beside him.

Unlacing his left boot, he eased out his aching foot, stripped off his grey woollen stocking and stared at his toe. It was hot, red and throbbing. As the cool mountain air caressed it, Gwilym began, tenderly, to rub away the pain. After a while he set his bare foot on the winter-worn grass and turned to get some food from his pack. Wrapped inside a linen cloth were oatcakes and a lump of cheese. He drank some water from a tin bottle in his coat pocket, saved until now as he had slaked his thirst at the many streams flowing beside the upland common, sipping their icy liquid from his cupped hands. The oatcakes were dry and crumbly, the cheese moist and salty.

How long it would take him to reach his destination he did not know. It was said the traveller could see signs of it and hear the noise of it miles before he reached it: the new Iron Town of Tydfil the Martyr. Gwilym was going there because he'd heard that Gwynfor the drover believed a strong lad like Gwilym could easily get a job in the town.

Gwilym needed a job. He was on his own now. His mother, Ellen, and baby sister Bronwen had died a year since.

'They died because we are poor,' his father William told Gwilym bitterly.

Their home had been a turf hut, a *caban unnos*, put up overnight on common land. It was the only way a poor man could gain land of his own, his father told him.

William had built it when he and Ellen were courting. It had been hard work to get the turf walls laid, clod on earth clod as if they were stones. Friends had helped. When the walls were over a man's height they laid branches to bridge the open space and topped it with more turf and furze branches to make a roof. A peat fire was set to make smoke, for if there was none to be seen rising from the chimney hole by daybreak someone else could claim the land.

The little turf hut had stood firm for years: it was the place where the children were born. The family took water from a stream, cooked over an open fire, slept on straw mattresses. To answer bodily calls they used the open ground and Nature cleansed the waste as it did that of cattle and sheep, foxes, badgers and all the other creatures of the countryside.

Gwilym was the eldest of the family. He'd had a brother, Ieuan, but he had died when he was two. The death of Ellen and her newest baby had broken Gwilym's father. He had laboured on until terrible frosts cut him down until he could do nothing but lie ill and shivering on his mattress. Gwilym cared for him as best he could.

Mrs Davies the miller's wife had given them broth. Her youngest daughter Jinny brought the bowls every day, covered by a plate to keep in the heat. For a week, mother and daughter had seen to it that the boy and his ailing father were fed. But neither the care nor the broth gave back William his will to live: he died quietly one night.

So that was how Gwilym came to be alone in the world and on the road to Iron Town. As he ate he thought back to his last hours at home.

He had packed the wooden cup and plate his father had made for him, and his mother's brown and cream checked shawl. The table, stools, bench and a soft chaff mattress tenderly made for Ellen (for it was softer than straw), had been offered to neighbours, who kindly insisted on paying, so as to fill Gwilym's money pouch. He carried the cooking pot and kettle to the mill that morning, for Mrs Davies.

Both she and Jinny had watched him as he walked away from the mill. Mrs Davies had wished the poor lad well, sorry that her husband had no job to offer him. Jinny, who was only a year younger than Gwilym, wondered if they would ever see each other again. When Gwilym turned at the bend to raise his hand in farewell, the corner of Mrs Davies's apron was held to her eyes.

The road led past the *caban unnos*, his humble turf-walled home. Gwilym sensed that without the warmth and care of a family living inside, it would crumble and return to the earth from which it was made.

Gwilym packed away his food, leaned back and looked up. Overhead, white clouds scudded across a pale sky. A buzzard circled and rose on lazy wings, higher and higher, until Gwilym could no longer see it. Grey clouds were massing in the east and a cold rush of wind urged him hurriedly to don his stocking and boot.

He had to find shelter before the rain reached him.

2

Gwilym had more money on him now than he'd ever seen in his life. It was in a leather drawstring pouch tied around his waist.

'Mind you keep it out of sight of footpads and other villains,' Mrs Davies had warned him.

Footpads and villains! Gwilym was startled but tried not to show his fear. 'Now here's an old waistcoat for you,' she went on. 'There's a special pocket stitched inside.'

She made him pack extra breeches and a shirt, cast-offs from her youngest son, though Gwilym protested that his pack would be more bulky.

'I'll be like a packhorse,' he complained cheerfully.

'You'll be glad of these to change into if you get wet.'

Mrs Davies had always been kind to him. There were tears in her eyes when he went to say goodbye. The miller, clothes dusted white with flour, had come down from the mill, saying, 'You'll take this as well and no argument,' and thrust a silver shilling roughly into Gwilym's hand.

'For the special pocket in your waistcoat,' his wife explained.

So he had put the clothes, wooden plate and cup, and the shawl inside his father's leather pack. On his feet were wooden-soled boots, in his left hand pocket a sharp knife in its leather sheath, in his right hand pocket a packet of food.

That was how he made ready for his great journey to Iron Town.

*   *   *

The track ahead rose higher as Gwilym trudged on. His left toe was not so painful, his stomach quietened by the oatcakes and cheese. Crows wheeled and complained overhead, warning of bad weather. The wind blew more chill. Gwilym glanced over his shoulder and saw dark grey rainclouds racing towards him. A slight scatter of raindrops tapped on his head, spurring him to a quicker pace. He had to find shelter before heavier rain fell.

As Gwilym topped the next rise he saw in the distance a group of wind-stunted trees. He began to run. Out of breath, he reached the trees. Crouching down under the tangle of branches, bare as yet of any leaves, he hunched his shoulders, pulled his jacket up over his head and prepared to be shrouded by the veil of rain sweeping towards him.

The sky darkened. A flash of forked lightning hit the ground a mile away, and the delayed crack of its thunder echoed eerily back from the mountains around.

All the birds had flown. No other soul was in sight. It was as if he was the only living thing in a desolate land. Huddled in his hiding place, Gwilym shuddered, not only with cold, as rain dripped about him.

But he was not the only being abroad. He heard a

faint rhythmic thudding. Nearer and nearer it came until a horseman rode into sight, galloping in Gwilym's direction.

Was this one of the villains Mrs Davies had warned him about? Was he a highwayman?

3

Gwilym crouched lower, hoping he could not be seen. But the rider had sharp eyes and made out the boy's dark form among the bare trunks of the trees.

The man raised his voice, but the wind snatched his words away. Coming closer, he reined in his chestnut mount and, as it fought the bit in its mouth, arching its neck against the restraint, he called out again.

'Get out from under those trees, lad, or you'll be struck by lightning!'

Gwilym was reluctant to move. The rider became impatient. 'Better be soaked through than struck dead!' he cried. 'Trust me, lad. Lightning will strike at the highest object in its path: these trees put you in danger.'

As the man spoke, his horse was becoming more restive, its eyes wide and fearful. Gwilym came out from his shelter.

'All alone, then? Where are you from? Where are you going?' asked the horseman.

Gwilym decided he need not fear him.

'To Iron Town, sir.'

'It's in the opposite direction I'm heading, otherwise you'd be welcome to ride with me,' said the man.

Oh, the temptation to give up the journey to Iron Town and ride on that magnificent horse!

'Can you give me a job, sir?' asked Gwilym, surprised at his own boldness.

'All I can offer is a ride,' smiled the horseman.

'Then I'll have to carry on my way. There's lots of work in Iron Town, I've been told,' said Gwilym, wiping his hand over his face to clear it of rain.

'I'm sorry I can't help you if that's the prospect ahead of you,' the man said soberly.

His mount was scraping the stony ground with restless hooves, as the rider turned in the saddle and pointed with his whip.

'Two miles on you'll see a track on the left that will take you to Cefn Glas farm. They may give you shelter. Hurry now away from here!'

He slackened the reins, touched the horse's sides with his heels, and set off swiftly along the track Gwilym had already travelled.

If only Gwilym, too, had a horse to ride: some company on this grim journey. He trudged on in the rain, soaked through to his skin. The track stretched on endlessly, water-logged and muddy.

With no sun by which to tell the time, Gwilym did not know what hour of the day it was when he at last found the rutted pathway leading to the farm.

He paused at the gate. The farmhouse was long and low. Rainwater sluiced off the stone tiles on its roof, gurgled along the guttering and into a drainpipe that clung to the wall with the help of a rusted metal bracket. There were two small windows tucked well up under the eaves, and an even smaller one further along, giving the building a hooded and sinister look. Below were another three, larger windows. A one-storey building extended on the left of the main farmhouse, its wide entrance made of rougher wood. From it came the odour of cows. In the darkening day the farmhouse's solid grey stones were hard and forbidding.

Gwilym looked up, blinking through the rain that dripped into his eyes. From the wide stone chimney the wind was snatching away smoke. Smoke signalled a fire. If there was a fire inside, somebody was there to tend it. But would he, a stranger, be made welcome to share its warmth?

A dog set up a clamour of barking as Gwilym fumbled to open the gate with fingers stiff with cold. A woman's face appeared at the big window, peering suspiciously, as his forlorn figure trudged across the yard to her door.

4

Gwilym raised his hand to knock. His knuckles were so cold he could not feel the impact. He put them under his armpits to bring them some warmth.

The woman cautiously opened the door an inch or two. At her heels another dog barked a warning.

'Oh! You're just a boy!' she exclaimed. 'What on earth are you doing out in weather like this?'

Gwilym's teeth were chattering.

'P . . . p . . . please c . . . c . . . can I have shelter until the storm is over?' he stuttered.

'Is anyone with you?'

'No.'

The woman opened the door wider.

'Come in.'

Gwilym hesitated, looking down at the dog which seemed determined to frighten him off.

'Don't mind Fly, she's all bark and no bite, but she's a great little watchdog,' said the woman. 'Come you into the kitchen and dry yourself. Then we'll see what we can do for you.'

Later, by the kitchen fire, with his jacket hung over the back of a chair, giving off steam as it dried, Gwilym sat contentedly. Warmth was coming back to his chilled hands as he cupped them around a pewter mug. It was filled with a delicious mixture of hot milk and honey.

The farm woman said, 'There was no point in asking you about anything when your teeth were chattering, but I'm asking now. What's your name? Why are you on your own? Where are you going?'

Gwilym knew she would not have asked any man or woman such direct questions. But her curiosity had to be satisfied, if only in payment for her kindness.

'I'm an orphan,' he said, remembering the word Mrs Davies had told him.

The woman made a sympathetic clucking noise.

Gwilym told her his name, where he was from and where he was going. He did not tell her about the money in his pouch and secret pocket. He wasn't daft.

'Heaven help you, lad,' the woman said. 'Whatever lies before you we cannot know, but you can sit with us for dinner when my boys come in, and you can sleep in the cowshed tonight.'

Like her dog, which was now lying quietly near the hearth, she had a bit of a bark about her. But Gwilym sensed a warm heart.

She told him about herself: a widow, she had three sons running the farm. They kept a few milk cows, sheep to sell for their fleeces or their meat. Some oats they grew for milling into flour and animal feed. Her name was Bessie Williams.

'Any horses?' asked Gwilym.

'Two,' said Mrs Williams. 'They're out at work with my sons.'

Looking closely at him she said, 'Boy, you are still soaking wet. Strip off those clothes.'

'NO!' exclaimed Gwilym.

'Don't be silly, boy. We'll dry them overnight. I'll give you something to put on instead.'

Gwilym waited apprehensively while Mrs Williams went upstairs. She returned with a grey and white striped nightshirt. 'Put this on,' she ordered, and left the room.

Gwilym struggled out of his clothes and dived into the voluminous depth of the nightshirt. His arm flailed about, seeking the armholes. When his head

19

emerged he was out of breath. The shirt was an arm's length too long for him. So were the sleeves. He rolled them up as far as his elbows and sat down again, tucking his feet into the folds of the shirt–tail. His money pouch was still tied around his waist. He had to be careful.

Mrs Williams came in when he'd had enough time to change, and set about hanging Gwilym's clothes on a string in front of the fire.

Gwilym eyed her closely over the rim of the mug as he finished drinking the sweet milk, but she did not attempt to feel in the pockets of his jacket, or to examine his waistcoat with its secret pocket. He relaxed.

After hanging up his sodden things Mrs Williams started to prepare *cawl*, a nourishing broth of vegetables and mutton.

'Thank you for the milk, Mrs Williams,' said Gwilym, setting the mug on the table.

The cauldron of *cawl* hung over a peat fire in a large stone fireplace. To the right of that, in a recess with a red curtain half hiding it, was a box bed. A door on the left led to stone stairs rising to the rooms above.

'Now you can make yourself useful,' said Mrs Williams. 'Help me peel these potatoes.'

She gave him a knife and tumbled a heap of freshly scrubbed potatoes into a bowl she placed in his lap. As he clumsily peeled great chunks of potato away with its skin, she rebuked him, 'Have you never peeled a potato before? You're wasting half of it. Do it like this.'

She swiftly shed a potato of its skin – peeled so thin he could almost see through it. 'The knife is keen, mind,' she warned.

By the time he had peeled his sixth and suffered a few more sharp words, Gwilym had almost mastered the task. A cut on his left forefinger bled and turned one potato pink. He hid it among the others and sucked the blood away.

A clock ticked on the wall. He'd seen one before, at the millhouse. He knew it told the time of day.

'What time is it, Mrs Williams?' he asked.

'There's a clock on the wall. Haven't you got eyes?' She had her back to him, adding carrots and turnips and onions to the cauldron.

Gwilym was silent. He couldn't read the clock. He was angry with himself for showing his ignorance.

Mrs Williams turned and saw his face. Glancing at the clock she said, 'It shows twenty five minutes after four o'clock but that old thing is usually slow.'

A savoury scent of *cawl* was filling the kitchen by the time the sons came in from the fields. They scraped mud from their boots on the iron bootscraper outside the door. When they entered, the boots rang sharply on the flag-stoned floor. Their rain-drenched coats they hung on wooden pegs.

They were sturdy, silent young men. If they were surprised to see him they did not show it.

'This is Gwilym. He's staying the night,' was all the explanation their mother gave. 'Gwilym, this is Dafydd, my eldest son, Hefin is the middle one and Siôn is the youngest.'

The brothers nodded to him in turn. They made no comment on the way he was dressed. The clothes in front of the fire gave the reason. But after their hunger had been satisfied by bowls of broth and hunks of barley bread, they eased back in their chairs, ready to hear any tale the boy might wish to tell.

Outside, the rain still lashed at the window. By the flickering light cast by the flames of the fire and in the friendly presence of the family, Gwilym felt ready to tell more of his story.

He spoke of how he'd lost his mother and young brother and sister. He told of his father's anguish and death, of selling his few possessions. He didn't tell of his sadness at leaving his friends, or his thoughts on last seeing his home.

All his listeners knew hardship. Dafydd rose from his chair, went to where his coat hung and fumbled in one of its pockets.

'For you, boy,' he said when he came back, and bent to put his gift into Gwilym's hand. 'You'll find that useful.'

Gwilym's face showed his gratitude.

'I'm off to bed once I've damped down this fire,' Dafydd went on. 'It's an early start for us all in this household.'

Hefin and Siôn scraped back their chairs and stood up.

'Hefin, set fresh straw for the boy to sleep on and show him where to go,' ordered Mrs Williams. 'It's in the cowshed you'll sleep tonight,' she told

Gwilym. 'Siôn, give him the blanket from the old chest by the window.'

She, it seemed, was to sleep in the box-bed, the warmest place in the house.

It was dark enough for a candle to be lit. Gwilym followed its unsteady flame as Hefin held it high. A heavy scent of cattle filled his nostrils. Candlelight gleamed on the lean flanks of three cows in their stall. They turned calm brown eyes towards the intruders, gently moving their jaws as they chewed the cud.

In the far corner of the shed, Hefin handed the candle to Gwilym, and forked down straw to cover the floor where Gwilym was to rest.

Siôn arrived, unfolding a large grey blanket and flinging it over the straw. It fell in lumpy billows.

'This will keep you warm,' he said.

'We'll take the candle with us in case you fall asleep before putting the candle out,' said Hefin.

The candle-flame disappeared, leaving Gwilym in the darkness with the softly breathing cows for company.

Down on his knees he set his pack as a pillow, lay on the blanket, covered himself, wriggling into the rustling, scratchy straw until he had worked it into a comfortable shape to fit his tired body. He was soon fast asleep.

5

A soft sound awakened Gwilym. The light in the cowshed was dim. He peered over the top of his blanket and saw Mrs Williams already about her day's tasks.

She was seated on a three-legged stool, her head pressed close to the side of a cow. Her hands gently but firmly squeezed the cow's udder to release a thin stream of milk into a wooden pail beneath.

Straw rustled as he moved. Mrs Williams glanced in his direction.

'So you're awake are you, Gwilym? Did you sleep well?'

'Yes,' Gwilym murmured.

'Into the kitchen with you. There'll be some of this milk and bread for breakfast.'

'Thank you, Mrs Williams,' said Gwilym, making no move to get up, for he was warm and comfortable.

Mrs Williams rose stiffly, picked up the pail and went towards the kitchen.

The milked cow lifted its head, dragged out a mouthful of sweet hay from the manger and chewed contentedly. It reminded Gwilym that he was hungry too.

From the kitchen came Mrs Williams' raised voice. 'Come on now, Gwilym. You've a long way to go and winter days are short. Get up now, there's a good boy.'

Gwilym stood, put on his boots and picked up the blanket, shaking it free of most of its clinging straw.

He clattered into the kitchen, holding the blanket awkwardly under his left arm and clutching at his nightshirt with his right hand so that he wouldn't tread on its length and trip himself up. He stood in the doorway, wondering what to do with the blanket.

The men seated at the table acknowledged him with a nod. They weren't as talkative as their mother. But they were all grinning widely at him. Why was that?

Gwilym felt foolish and scowled. Hefin rose, went to the mantelpiece over the hearth, picked up something and handed it to Gwilym. It was a comb.

'There's straw in your hair,' he said.

Gwilym dropped his hold on the nightshirt and hastily dragged the comb through his hair, shedding straw onto the floor and wincing as the teeth of the comb caught in stubborn tangles.

Busy at the hearth, Mrs Williams asked him if he had shaken out the blanket.

'Fold it up and put it into the chest under the window,' she ordered.

Gwilym gave the three young men more quiet amusement as he struggled to fold the blanket. He managed it at last, hot with embarrassment, as he closed the lid of the chest.

'The rain has slackened off. You won't get so wet today,' Dafydd told him.

Gwilym's clothes were thoroughly dry.

'Here you are. You can put these on now,' said Mrs Williams handing them to him.

Under the modest folds of the nightshirt Gwilym

slipped off his boots and donned his breeches and the rest of his garments. Clad in his own clothes he felt more at ease. He ate his breakfast with enjoyment. Mrs Williams gave him a helping as large as those she gave her grown sons.

'Its time for you to be on your way again, lad,' said Dafydd, looking at the clock. 'Go back to the Drovers' Way you were on yesterday. Keep on it, going towards the rising sun, and you'll reach the highroad, the turnpike. There'll be carts on the road. You may get a ride on one of them.'

As he was preparing to leave, Gwilym asked what animals they had on the farm.

'Cows, as you've seen, sheep, two pigs, hens, two horses,' said Siôn.

'I like horses,' said Gwilym. 'Where are they then?'

'In the stables across the yard,' said Siôn.

'I know a poem about horses,' said Hefin suddenly and began to recite, eyes shut to help him remember.

> *See the white fleet-footed steed,*
> *Lively, joyous of good breed;*
> *Slender flanks, hair fine as down*
> *And silky mane like a maiden's gown.*

'Did you make that up?' asked Gwilym, impressed.

'No. It is an old poem written long ago. I wish I had written it though,' answered Hefin.

Mrs Williams stopped her work to listen to her

son. 'He writes poetry himself,' she said. 'Good poems they are, too.'

Hefin looked surprised. It wasn't often that his mother praised him for his poems. More often she berated him, saying he was neglecting work in day-dreaming.

'I saw a fine horse yesterday,' said Gwilym. He described the horseman. 'He was in a dreadful rush,' he added.

'That would have been Dr James and Blazer,' said Siôn. 'Someone must have been at death's door, for the doctor always rides when he has to get to a patient in particular distress. Blazer is swift and sure-footed.'

A culf of fresh bread and lump of cheese had found their way into Gwilym's coat pocket.

'Thank you, Mrs Williams,' he said, grateful for her thoughtfulness. 'Can you tell me anything about Iron Town, then?'

'It's a town that's growing fast, so I've heard,' said Dafydd.

'It's a rough place,' said Siôn. 'I wouldn't want to go there.'

'There's jobs there, though,' said Gwilym.

'Oh, there's jobs all right. Good money too, for those who'll take the risk. But I'm not tempted. I'm staying on the farm,' Siôn continued. 'You're not as likely to get burned and maimed on a farm.'

6

'Burned! Maimed!' exclaimed Gwilym.

'Furnaces,' said Siôn. 'Where they make the iron. They say the heat blinds you.'

'Enough of that,' interrupted Mrs Williams. She did not want to frighten the boy.

Maimed! Burned! Blinded! What kind of work was it that wrecked your body while you earned your living? The warning scared Gwilym, but what other choice did he have? There was no work here on the farm for anyone but the family, Mrs Williams had told him that already.

There was no work back home, either; not that he had any home to go back to. He had to move on. Plenty of jobs in Iron Town, the drover had said. Perhaps he could find some that were a bit safer.

He'd go on to Iron Town as planned. Find out for himself.

It was eight o'clock when he set off again. Mrs Williams told him that was what the clock in the kitchen said it was, 'give or take ten minutes, fast or slow.'

She watched him go. Gwilym saw tears in her eyes, but it was because she had been peeling onions, he decided. As he looked back, the little window which had given the farmhouse a sinister look the day before, now seemed to be giving him a friendly wink.

The brothers were about their daily chores. Hefin was feeding the pigs, Dafydd harnessing the plough-horses in the stable. Siôn, with a sheepdog at his heels, was setting off for the fields. They called out their goodbyes and good wishes as his small figure walked out of the yard and out of their lives.

As Gwilym left the farm track and regained the Drovers' Way, he thought about that last warning.

'It's a long, lonely track you'll be on. Watch out for the Devil's Staircase,' Dafydd had told him.

His pathway entered a narrow valley, shrouded in morning mist. Rough, bleak mountains rose on both sides. The track clung to the curve on the eastern slopes. Sometimes he was walking uphill, sometimes down. Gradually each rise became higher.

The mist he had seen from a distance now enveloped him. He moved through its clammy dampness like a small ghost.

If only he had a horse, like the Squire's hunter or the Doctor's muscled cob. He walked on. If only he had a workaday horse like the ones back on the farm.

His imagination leapt ahead of him. I'll tame a pony, he thought. I'll tame a pony. Ride him bareback. When I get to Iron Town I'll maybe sell it. That'll give me some more money to live on until I find a job.

He was walking along, still in the mist, when the path dropped away. He slipped but regained his balance. He could see no further than his nose. Veils of mist shifted before his eyes. He stepped forward more cautiously. His feet felt level ground, then he slipped again as the path dipped repeatedly.

The track was muddy, rutted, scoured by heavy downpours of winter rain. Seven times Gwilym slithered and slid downwards until the last and longest slide. His boots slipped from under him. Down he sat with a painful bump.

He got to his feet, rubbing his behind, glad he had not landed in the worst of the mud. He glanced back at the natural steps which loomed up in the gloom behind him.

'The Devil's Staircase!' he exclaimed aloud.

The track ahead levelled out. Stone-strewn and muddy, it threaded its way through tussocks of yellow grass across the floor of the valley, along and around the sloping shoulder of the mountain.

Mist thinned as the watery sun rose. Now Gwilym scanned the valley for signs of ponies. Mountain ponies, the strong tough breed that would still be clad in their heavy winter coats at this time of year.

Several heaps of dung showed where the herd had grazed. Gwilym went over to one and kicked at it to see if it was fresh, to gauge whether the ponies had been there recently. It was fresh. He scraped his boot clean on the grass and walked on.

Some miles farther on the wind scattered the remnants of the mist and brought with it a familiar scent.

Ponies!

7

A herd of twelve mares and one stallion was grazing the valley floor ahead. One pony was separated from the others, intent on seeking a more succulent patch of grass among the winter-withered turf.

Gwilym stood still. The wind was blowing in his direction so the pony had not scented him. Reaching into his pocket for the hunk of barley bread, Gwilym tore some off and moved slowly towards it.

The pony, a young bay mare, shaggy in its winter coat, lifted its head and saw him. Gwilym stayed still. Unconcerned, it went on cropping the unappetising grass. Gwilym moved closer, holding out the bread in his hand. The pony kept wary brown eyes on him. But it too stepped closer, still grazing.

Gwilym was within a step or two of the pony, knowing that any sudden movement would scare the animal back to the herd.

The wind shifted slightly, wafting the smell of bread towards the pony. As it lifted its dark brown head, its nostrils flared. The temptation to go forward was almost overwhelming but Gwilym stayed motionless.

It was the pony who moved. Gwilym held out the piece of bread on his flattened palm, not wanting the pony's teeth to catch his fingers. It sniffed the bread, gathering it with outstretched lips. It stepped closer. It wanted more.

Soon Gwilym was able to stroke its soft muzzle and tickle it behind its ears, talking softly, delighted at his success. The pony shook its heavy mane and

Gwilym feared it would trot back to the herd, but the prospect of another piece of bread kept it close.

With his hand on its neck Gwilym quietly moved to its side, gently grasped a bunch of wiry mane in his left hand and flung himself over its back, scrambling to sit astride.

Startled, the animal jerked up its head and set off wildly in the direction of its companions.

Desperately, Gwilym clung on. His knees pressed close to the pony's flanks, his body bent low, both hands entangled in the young mare's mane.

His pack bumped heavily on his back.

This was thrilling! He had never moved so fast in his life.

8

He must not fall off. All his muscles and sinews strained to keep him on the pony's back. The other ponies scattered as Gwilym's mount raced towards them and through the herd.

Suddenly the pony halted, braced its forelegs, head down. Gwilym slid halfway down its neck, his behind in the air, but he stayed on.

Before he could be too pleased with himself, the mare gave a sharp buck with its hind legs, unseating him completely. As he fell to the ground it gave another buck to make sure it had got rid of him, and trotted briskly away, head held high.

Gwilym sat up, bruised but exhilarated. The cheeky way the pony had dealt with him made him laugh. Some of his possessions had been shaken out. It took him some time to pick them up and repack them.

By then the herd had gathered together, the cheeky mare safely in their midst, with the stallion circling them, defiantly facing Gwilym. Reluctantly Gwilym shouldered his burden and turned to continue his journey.

His mind was on the pony for many miles after he left the herd. He would be better prepared if he met up with other ponies on the way. He would make a halter to capture one; maybe make a rope as a halter. Use rough grass, maybe, twisted and bound and spliced together.

His legs by now were moving at an easy pace. He had been walking for so long it seemed that the track was coming up to meet his feet. Overhead, bright clouds raced and flocks of birds rose, wheeled and swooped in the joy of flight. Trudging along on his solid earth-bound legs, Gwilym envied them.

At last the valley ended and its track met a broader road. This must be the turnpike. Which way was he to go? There was no-one to ask. Gwilym looked up at the sun, turned east, turned right, and set off again.

The turnpike road may have been wider but it was still hard going. Deep and muddy ruts showed that carts had dug their wheels into its yielding surface. He would have to be careful where he trod in case he turned on his ankle.

The land around was flatter, softer, greener. Hedges of hawthorn, blackthorn, hazel and holly bordered the road. Gwilym noticed there were still many hazelnuts, brown and ready for gathering, in the hedge. He filled his pockets with them and ate them, walking along. Some he cracked open with his teeth. Some he had to smash open with a stone on stone.

The day was bright and clear. His feet were hardening to the task of walking mile after mile. His pack felt light and his spirit was high.

In the fields beyond the hedges he glimpsed black cattle. They must be the cattle the drovers took to market. Gwynfor the Drover had told his father how they drove over hundreds of miles to market.

The sound of hammering came from the distance, followed by a loud shout and coarse laughter.

9

On the road ahead was a group of men, laughing at a small man who was hopping about. Large stones were dumped on the side of the road. The men were working on them, hammering them smaller. These small stones were piled into another heap. What was the point of that, thought Gwilym. Were they daft?

The small man was holding his left hand under his armpit, nursing its hurt from where he had hit it with his hammer. His workmates were still grinning about his clumsiness when Gwilym trudged up to them.

The stone-breakers greeted him in friendly fashion.

'Where are you from, boy?' asked one of the older men. 'On your own, are you?'

'Where are you off to?' asked another man.

Gwilym looked from one to another, undecided about how much to say. The other men had stopped teasing the clumsy one and turned all their attention to him. It was his turn to ask a question.

'What are YOU doing then?'

'Can't you see what we're doing?' asked a red-headed young man.

'Breaking stones,' said Gwilym sharply. 'It's what you're going to do with them I can't see.'

Red-head laughed. 'We're mending the road, lad. See those potholes, big enough to swim in, some of them are, after a winter's rain. We fill them up with the small stones, level them all off; make the road smooth and easy for carts and carriages, so people won't tip out and break their heads.'

'You've a long road to mend,' said Gwilym, thinking of the weary miles he'd walked.

'We repair the part of the turnpike road that runs through our parish, that's all. Men from other parishes have to do the same to their patch of road.'

'Some are doing a better job than others,' said Gwilym. 'I've travelled rough road to get here and I don't see that this is much different.'

'You cheeky monkey!' said Red-head.

The older man had set down his hammer and unwrapped a large white cloth, laying it carefully on a flat stone. He uncovered a chunk of cheese and a hunk of bread. He cut off a piece of cheese and with it still stuck to the knife, put it in his mouth.

'You'll cut yourself, Dan,' warned Red-head.

'Not if I'm careful,' answered Dan, chewing contentedly like Mrs Williams's cow. 'You hungry, boy?'

'I've got food,' said Gwilym, to show his independence.

'Eat it with us now,' said a kindly-looking man in a checked waistcoat. 'It's time for us to have a break, isn't it, Dan? Dan always knows when it's time.'

'He knows because he's the only one of us with a timepiece,' said Red-head.

'We have a break to eat at 12 o'clock,' explained the kind man. 'What time is it, Dan?'

Dan dragged at a watch-chain that threaded through his brown waistcoat buttonhole and disappeared into a small pocket. Out came a silver timepiece. He examined it closely.

'Twelve o'clock. It's time,' he declared.

As Dan had already started his break, Gwilym thought the timepiece must be like Mrs Williams's clock, telling the time 'give or take ten minutes fast or slow.'

The rest of the men dropped their hammers and gathered together, some sharing what they had with others. The waistcoat man, whose name was Eli, had brought apples.

'Quench your thirst, these do,' he said, holding one out for Gwilym to take.

It was a bit withered from being kept over winter, in a box in Eli's kitchen. Gwilym bit into it. It was juicy and sweet. He enjoyed it, and the company, for the men were a cheerful crew.

'Off to Market Town, are you?' asked Dan.

Gwilym chewed the apple. He didn't have to tell these men anything. What he did was none of their business.

'Don't say anything to anyone unless you have to,' his father used to tell him when he chattered on too much about his doings.

His mother taught him songs. His father didn't mind his singing; not until his mother died. Gwilym was helping his father clear the potato patch a few weeks after the funeral and, without realising what he was doing, Gwilym had begun to sing.

'Stop that!' his father had shouted at him, his face contorted.

Gwilym was frightened. What had he done but sing his mother's favourite song? Flinging down his hoe, his father had walked off, shoulders hunched. He seemed very alone.

When he came back to his work Gwilym said softly, 'Sorry, Dada. Sorry I made you angry.'

His father touched him gently on the shoulder. 'It wasn't anger you saw in my face, son. It was grief.'

How he missed his dear Dada and Ma and the children. His family. None of these roadmen could compare with his father. But he should answer one question. It was only polite.

'I'm going where the next step takes me,' said Gwilym at last.

'We've a bright lad here,' said Red-head. 'He gives an answer that's no answer.'

Dan-with-the-timepiece said, 'Your next step takes you to Market Town if you stay on this road. Watch out for robbers, mind.'

Gwilym finished eating his apple and threw the core behind the hedge.

'I'll be off then,' he said, picking up his pack.

Mockingly he took exaggeratedly careful steps away from the men, along the road they said they had repaired.

Laughter and cries of 'You cheeky young devil!' followed him as he went on his way in the direction of Market Town.

10

He'd been stupid. He should have asked the road menders to tell him how long it would take to walk to Market Town. Gwilym trudged on. The road was scored with the parallel lines of cart tracks. He hoped to have a ride on a cart now that he was on the turnpike road. But not a cart could be seen; no riders either.

The weather-stunted trees of the mountains had long been left behind. Now Gwilym walked under overhanging branches of oak, sycamore and ash. Through the tangle of twigs he saw that the sun was casting a rose glow over the sky: dusk was falling.

Gwilym's legs were tiring. His muscles ached. Soon he would have to find a place to spend the night. A mile farther on, the road took a sharp turn and began to descend. A wider view came in sight. In the distance he could see the roof of a building almost hidden among trees. Remembering the welcome he'd had at Cefn Glas farm, Gwilym quickened his pace. Here was somewhere he could rest.

The road levelled and straightened. Far off was a dark moving figure. With thudding hooves and a flying cloak, a horse and rider galloped in his direction. Gwilym stood aside for them to pass, not wanting to be struck by the horse's frantic action. But it did not reach him. The animal was pulled up sharply, its head jerked back cruelly, its mouth open, gasping for breath. The rider, who did not notice him, slid to the ground and led his mount quickly out of sight. They must be going to the house whose roof he'd seen.

The rough way the rider had treated his horse made Gwilym angry. When he reached the place where horse and rider had disappeared he saw that the building was not a house or a farm but a squalid-looking inn. It was not a welcoming inn. It had a secretive air about it. An old and dirty sign showed it was the White Rock Tavern. Gwilym moved cautiously towards a grimy window and peered in to a candle-lit room

The horseman, still in his riding cloak, was standing talking urgently to an aproned man whom Gwilym took to be the innkeeper. They were arguing. The rider was slapping his boot impatiently with a riding whip.

It didn't seem too good a moment to interrupt them with a request for a place to stay the night.

Gwilym crept away, around the side of the inn. If he could find the stables he could bed down in the straw as he had done in the farm. A stamp of hoof on stone led him to cross the dark yard and slip into the stable. The horse he had seen raised a frightened head and started back, pulling on its tether. He spoke softly, soothing the animal with gentle words. Whip strokes marked its sweating hide.

The back door of the inn opened, spilling light onto the flagstoned yard. Gwilym hastened to the farthest and darkest corner of the stables, crouching down.

'You're a fool if you don't come into this venture with me,' he heard the rider say. 'There's good pickings in Iron Town.'

The innkeeper's grumbling voice muttered in dissent. 'All very well for you to say that, Jed. You'll take your share and be off. I'm tied to this place.'

'Sleep on it, Nathan,' said Jed. 'I'll have to stay the night anyway for I won't get another mile out of Bess until she's rested. Get some food on the table while I attend to her.'

Gwilym heard the sound of water being pumped. The stable door was kicked open and Jed put a slopping bucket in front of his tired horse.

When he left, Gwilym pondered on what he had heard. Pickings? What did the rider mean? Thieving; it had to be. Good pickings didn't have an honest sound about it. Gwilym decided he would have to move out early in the morning. He didn't want to risk being discovered. He didn't want whip strokes across *his* back.

Dreams of thieves and robbers tramping the roads to Iron Town filled his uneasy sleep.

11

It was dark and very cold when he awoke. The horse was standing, head low, sleeping. Gwilym picked up his pack and made his way quietly out of the yard, back on to the turnpike road. He stumbled many times in the pre-dawn darkness in his haste to put as many miles as possible between himself and the tavern.

It was still in the early hours when he arrived in Market Town. As he walked down the wide main street, he saw on either side neat, grey stone houses, shops selling farm implements and even a shop with ladies' hats and mantles in its window. There was a butcher's shop and one with fat round cheeses on display. The shopkeepers were taking down the shutters and opening the doors for business.

There were taverns and a coaching inn with a wide archway leading to stables where the coach horses were changed. His Dada had told him about such things. 'They say some people want to go as far as London,' he'd said. 'They make their wills before they go, in case they have an accident.' Gwilym had asked why they wanted to go if it was so dangerous. 'Business,' his Dada had replied.

Women in long skirts and warm woollen shawls hurried about the street, popping into one shop and another, pausing to greet friends and exchange gossip. One young woman wore a pretty strawchip bonnet, tied under her chin with ribbon. A long brown cloak half-concealed the basket she carried on her arm. As she passed, Gwilym wished his mother could have had a bonnet and cloak like that.

Strong muscled horses with hairy hooves pulled along two-wheeled and four-wheeled carts. There was now an air of commercial bustle about the street.

'Is it market day?' Gwilym asked a passing shopper.

'No, lad,' was the reply. 'If it was market day you wouldn't be able to move for the cattle and sheep and horses.'

Gwilym wandered on, gazing around in amazement.

A cart pulled up in front of the Black Ox Inn as Gwilym came up. The carter jumped down, flinging the reins of the team of horses over the brass rail at the front of the cart. From the back he began to unload barrels of ale.

'Need any help?' asked Gwilym, hopeful of earning a penny or two.

'He's got help,' said a sour voice behind him. 'I'm helping him. Get you off from here.'

Gwilym turned to face a black-haired youth. He was scowling.

'Mind now, Jethro. Don't start any trouble,' said the carter.

'Get off with you,' growled Jethro under his breath. He brushed against Gwilym, deliberately bumping him with his shoulder so that Gwilym stumbled, almost knocking over a cask.

'Clumsy oaf,' sneered Jethro. He shouldered the cask the carter reached down to him and swaggered into the dark depths of the inn. Gwilym had to admit he could not even have lifted the cask, let alone carry it. He could have rolled it, though.

Wandering farther down the street, he smelled something delicious: freshly baked bread. He stopped. Head up, like a dog picking up a scent, he sniffed deeply. It led him down an alleyway. And there was the source: a bakehouse. He lingered in the doorway to watch.

Three men worked there. Loaves of bread, plump, brown and crisp-crusted, were being shovelled from the back of the brick oven on wooden instruments with paddle-like blades at the end of long poles. Everything was coated in a thin dusting of flour. The warmth given off by the ovens was comforting.

One of the bakers, a small man, noticed him.

'Followed the smell, did you?' he asked.

Gwilym nodded.

'You're not the first one. Want a loaf?'

'How much?'

'Depends on what you want.'

'A job,' said Gwilym tentatively.

'No spare jobs here. You'll have to go to Iron Town for a job.'

'That's where I'm going, really,' admitted Gwilym. 'I was just looking for something to fill in . . .'

'Fill in, is it?' interrupted the man. 'Fill these baskets for me and you'll earn yourself a fresh crust.'

So Gwilym put his belongings under a trestle table and set to. Ieuan told him to take baked loaves from the racks where they were cooled, and put them into cloth-lined baskets.

'Where do these go now?' he asked.

'We deliver them to our customers,' said Ieuan. 'Two white loaves to Dr Trefor's house; two brown loaves to Mrs Jenkins the landlady; one small cob to Mrs Evans, Cross Street; two white to Mrs Williams Sheep Lane . . .' the baker paused. 'You can deliver some for me.'

Gwilym had stopped listening to these details which, to the baker, seemed important. Now he had been offered a chance to prolong his job.

A clatter of hooves and a rattle of wheels announced the arrival of the delivery cart, drawn by a black pony with a white blaze.

'Hand up those baskets,' called the driver.

Gwilym had never seen anyone who looked so cheerful. Working for a baker, driving a smart cart harnessed to a lively pony, the man had good reason to be happy.

As he handed up the baskets, Gwilym said, 'I'm doing deliveries too. Can I have a lift?'

'You can use Shanks' pony to do your deliveries,' answered the driver, winking at Ieuan.

Gwilym looked around. There was not another pony in sight.

'Where's Shanks then?' he asked.

44

Both men laughed.

'Don't see anything to laugh about,' Gwilym retorted.

'Only you, lad,' responded the baker.

Gwilym felt himself go red in the face. The driver relented.

'I'll be going the farthest, you'll be doing local deliveries – on foot. Shanks are legs. Going on Shanks' pony means walking on your own two legs,' he explained.

Gwilym glowered. He'd remember those words.

The driver slapped the reins, clicked his tongue and the pony pulled the cart down the alley on their way to the outskirts of Market Town.

The baker handed Gwilym a basket of fresh white loaves.

'Take these to Llewelyn Street. Numbers one to seven on the left hand side, and eight, nine, ten, eleven, twelve and fourteen on the right.'

'What about number thirteen?' said Gwilym. He had pushed his forearm through the handle of the basket and picked it up. It was heavy.

'There's no number thirteen. It's an unlucky number, so some folks think,' said Ieuan.

'Where's Llewelyn Street?' asked Gwilym.

'Down the alley, turn left until you get to the cobbler's shop, cross the road, go left again a step or two, then turn right. You'll be in Llewelyn Street. Mind you bring the basket back or you won't get your crust,' warned the baker.

Crust! Gwilym could eat one whole loaf with no

trouble. He could eat a whole loaf from the basket and keep on going and not come back . . . He could keep going on Shanks' pony right out of town. He could take all the loaves . . . If he did, he'd be a thief. His Dada and Ma wouldn't want him to be a thief. Anyway, he had to go back because he'd left his pack at the bakehouse.

With these thoughts he walked briskly in the direction the baker had directed. A sleepy-eyed maidservant answered the door at number one. At number nine there was no answer to his knock, so rather than leave the household with no bread, he left a loaf on a window sill and hoped it would not rain. He soon emptied the basket. The mystery of the missing number thirteen puzzled him even more now. There was no space between twelve and fourteen where the unlucky number could have been.

So fourteen was really thirteen. Anyone living in fourteen, right next to twelve must surely realise that they were living in an unlucky house, whatever was on the door. People in Llewelyn Street must be daft.

Gwilym wended his way back to the bakehouse. Around the corner of the unlucky street, he and his empty basket bumped into someone rushing past. It was Jethro. He eyed the baker's basket and then recognised Gwilym.

'You again! You clumsy little job-stealer. Give me that!' he shouted.

Tearing the basket from Gwilym's desperate grasp he made off down the street.

How could Gwilym go back to Ieuan without the basket? Would the baker believe it had been stolen? Would he give him the promised crust of bread? After all, he had delivered all the loaves, and he was hungry. Back to the bakehouse he went.

Jethro was there, talking to the baker, handing him the basket with such an air of ingratiating virtue that Gwilym wanted to thump him. He hung back, not knowing what tale Jethro was spinning. Bread or no bread, he had to collect his pack. He walked forward.

'Seems I'm lucky to get this back,' said Ieuan, taking the basket.

'I was bringing it back when he took it off me,' said Gwilym indignantly.

'He banged into me, deliberate,' said Jethro. 'He's going around taking jobs off me, and I live here! He's a stranger!'

'Collect your things, boy,' said the baker.

It was no use arguing. Jethro's look of triumph was hard to take.

12

More and more people were about the town. More carts drove by, pulled by strong horses straining into their horse collars, hooves slipping on the cobbles. Above the clatter of wheels and shouts of carters, Gwilym heard a loud clanging of metal on metal.

He went in the direction of the sound. It came from a side lane. The noise was coming from a forge.

The smell of hot iron attacked his nostrils and made him gasp. Flames lit up the gloom of the smithy. The stone walls were hung with strange tools. Some he recognised as tongs and hammers of all sizes.

The blacksmith was working at the anvil. He was hammering and shaping a red-hot and most peculiar shoe. It was smaller than any horseshoe Gwilym had seen. On the floor in the corner was a heap of similar iron shoes. As the blacksmith paused to wipe sweat from his forehead he saw Gwilym loitering in the doorway. He held the heavy hammer in his hand as lightly as if it was a piece of straw.

'Where've you sprung from?' he asked.

Reheating the shoe on the burning coals of the forge's fire gave the blacksmith a spare moment to question his visitor.

'From the baker's,' said Gwilym.

The blacksmith snorted with annoyance. He knew an evasive answer when he heard one. He was not going to let Gwilym off.

'You're not from around here.' He said it as a statement of fact. 'Are you?' he added almost accusingly.

Gwilym was silent. Should he tell? He'd been asked if he was from 'around here'. He wasn't: 'No,' he said.

The blacksmith snorted again and resumed his work. Gwilym watched the hammer rise and fall, striking swift and hard on the shoe which was softened by the fire and glowing scarlet with retained heat. Sparks flew with each stroke.

'What are you making?' asked Gwilym.

'Why should I tell you?' said the blacksmith, letting fly with a particularly hard thump of his hammer.

Gwilym was silent.

'I've come from Cefn Glas Farm,' he said at last, not telling about the stable at White Rock Tavern and his suspicions about Jed.

The blacksmith acknowledged the concession with a nod.

'What do you think I'm making?'

'Horseshoes, I suppose, but they must be for terrible small horses,' suggested Gwilym.

'Haven't you seen shoes for cattle, boy?'

'No,' said Gwilym.

Shoes on cows? Was the man daft?

'Haven't you noticed cattle's hooves are different to horses'?'

As Gwilym's face showed he did not understand, the blacksmith explained.

'They've got cloven hooves, split in two parts. So we make two for each hoof. Two small shoes for each cloven hoof.'

Horses needed metal shoes to prevent their hooves splitting from contact with hard ground. Gwilym knew that. But cows grazed on soft ground and did no work as horses had to do.

'. . . two shoes on each hoof; four shoes for a horse, eight shoes for a cow,' went on the blacksmith.

All the while he was hammering, turning, re-heating the shoe he was working on. Finally the finished shoe was dropped into a bucket of water, hissing and spitting as it cooled. Then it was drawn out and flung onto the heap in the corner of the smithy.

Gwilym was amazed. There were enough shoes in the blacksmith's workshop to shoe all the cattle in Wales.

'Our Mrs Jenkins' cow didn't wear shoes,' said Gwilym, remembering one of his kind neighbours who brought milk for them when his mother was ill.

'Your Mrs Jenkins' cow didn't have to walk to Smithfield,' said the blacksmith.

A look of incomprehension had fixed on Gwilym's face.

'London,' said the blacksmith. 'Smithfield is a meat market. There's a lot of people there. London people like beef. The cattle are here, the people are there. Do the people come in droves over the border to Wales to buy their beef . . .?'

What was the man talking about? Droves of people?

'No, the cattle go in droves over the border to London, thousands of them.'

'Where are they then?' asked Gwilym. 'I can see you're hard at it making cattle shoes but I don't see any cattle you say will need them.'

The blacksmith stopped his work on a straight piece of iron he was to shape into a new shoe and looked at Gwilym.

'For a little 'un you've got plenty of cheek,' said the blacksmith.

'My Dada told me always to ask questions. Questions, questions, he used to say. Ask questions. Sometimes you'll get daft answers but sometimes you'll learn something useful,' said Gwilym, defending himself.

'Where's your father?'

'Dead,' said Gwilym. 'So's my Ma.'

He said it quickly to get it out of the way so it wouldn't hurt so much.

The blacksmith went back to his work. He was silent for a while but the noise of his work filled the silence. Heating, hammering, turning, striking the white hot iron, shaping it into another, oddly dainty half-shoe, then cooling it to be flung onto the growing pile in the corner.

'You'll see the cattle in August,' said the blacksmith at last. 'There's shoes for 400 beef cattle over there,' he indicated the pile. 'Four hundred cattle, eight hundred shoes. This lot is for Dafydd Tomos the Drover.

'He'll bring his cattle here for shoeing and he'll join up with other drovers in August. Then they'll all be off to London. Thousands of cattle there'll be, driven along the Drovers' Way. Then there's the Drovers' Road or Welsh Way: there are different names for the roads they travel but they all lead to London.'

'I've come along a Drovers' Way,' said Gwilym.

He told the blacksmith about the time he sheltered from the storm and how he slipped and slid down the Devil's Staircase.

'For a little 'un you've plenty of go in you,' said the blacksmith. Gwilym didn't like being called a little 'un. 'If you've walked all that way it's no

51

wonder your boots are wearing out,' said the blacksmith, looking down at Gwilym's clog boots. 'I could shoe you, if you like.'

Gwilym didn't fancy having red hot plates hammered onto his feet.

'Shoe ME?' he cried out.

13

The blacksmith was making a joke, but he wasn't the kind of man who smiled while he made it.

'Your clogs are worn down. They need metal studs on the soles. They'd make the clogs last longer.'

Gwilym twisted his right foot to look at the thick wooden soles of his boots. They were scraped, scratched and deeply scored by the stones he'd walked on.

'They're not too bad,' he claimed.

The blacksmith sighed a deep sigh.

'Take 'em off,' he said. 'OFF!' he thundered as Gwilym hesitated.

Hastily Gwilym sat on a pile of sacks and fumbled with the bootlaces.

'How much will this cost me?' he asked. 'I didn't ask to have it done, did I?'

'Blow the fire with the bellows,' ordered the blacksmith, nodding towards the round leather air bag with a metal spout that hung near the fire.

Gwilym took off the boots and handed them to the blacksmith. Then he seized the bellows and vigorously pumped air into the base of the fire. The dulling cinders glowed bright scarlet again.

From a wooden box on the grimy window sill the blacksmith delicately picked out blunt-headed metal studs. Swiftly he tapped them into a half circle at the toe and heel of each boot.

'You'll get many more miles out of them now,' he said, handing the clogs back to Gwilym, who was now warming his feet by the fire.

'Thank you. How much do I owe?'

'You brightened up the fire for me so I'll let you off paying this time,' said the blacksmith. 'You could say I did it for your Ma and Da. You're a good enough lad. They'd be proud of you, I'm sure.'

'Thank you again then,' said Gwilym. His eyes were smarting a bit. 'I'm going now,' he said. He picked up his pack and left the smithy so fast the blacksmith had no time to wish him well.

Outside there was no-one near so he leaned against the rough stone wall and sniffed hard to stop his eyes from watering.

There were times he did not mind being all alone. It was exciting. It was an adventure. But there were times, like now, with the gruff, kind, blacksmith, when he thought of friends back home. Mr Davies the miller and his wife, and Jinny, Mrs Jenkins and her sons Tomos and Meredith; could he have stayed with them? No, he would have been an extra mouth to feed. Their kindness would have been strained. It was better to be as he was, alone but independent.

Dada and Ma would be proud of me, the blacksmith

said. He hadn't thought of it like that. Gwilym straightened up and walked towards the street.

'You still here, job stealer?'

It was the snarling voice of Jethro.

14

Gwilym spun around. Jethro seemed taller and tougher than before. His black eyebrows were drawn together in a fiercesome frown.

'I'm doing no harm. Why are you picking on me?' complained Gwilym.

'Sneaking around the place . . . It's you are doing the picking! Picking up jobs. There's not many jobs around here and what jobs there are, are mine!' declared Jethro.

'They must be odd jobs for you to be able to do them,' snapped Gwilym.

Jethro's right fist shot forward and punched Gwilym's chin. His jaw shifted sideways, three inches at least so it seemed. He staggered back against the wall. Jethro lowered his fist but kept it clenched in case Gwilym showed signs of fight.

Gwilym was busy fingering his chin, moving it carefully from right to left. I must look like a cow chewing the cud, he thought.

It was no good arguing with words when Jethro argued with his fists. If only I was bigger, taller, heavier, had more muscles . . . if only. Gwilym went back to words.

'Don't know what you're so bothered about,' said Gwilym speaking in a mumble because his jawbone was sore. 'I'm not stopping in this town. I'm on my way out of here anyway.'

'Go on then,' urged Jethro. 'I'll kick you halfway to wherever you're going!'

Gwilym shifted the pack on his shoulder.

'What's in that pack. Let's have a look,' said Jethro, changing tack.

'Mind your own business,' said Gwilym.

'Let's take a look,' repeated Jethro. He grabbed Gwilym by the collar.

'Thought you wanted to kick me out of town,' said Gwilym, his neck muffled to the chin in Jethro's grip.

'After I've seen what's in that pack. Give it here!' demanded Jethro.

'NO!' Gwilym cried out, twisting and struggling in Jethro's strong young grasp.

Jethro kicked him on the shin.

'Here's one kick to start with,' he said.

Gwilym's anguished yell alerted the blacksmith who came out into the lane, hammer in hand.

'Let the boy go, you young ruffian, Jethro!' he shouted.

Jethro looked back, surprised.

Gwilym slipped from his clutching fingers and ran into the High Street. Past shops, past houses, taverns; he ran until he was out of the town, his feet clattering with the sharp sound of his newly-studded clog boots. He ran until he had no breath left.

His chest heaving, he dropped his pack onto the

grass verge and sank down beside it. His heart pounded and his legs trembled. Gradually his breathing eased. Now he had time to notice pain.

He rolled down his stocking to examine the damage Jethro's kick had done to his leg. The thick wool had cushioned the kick slightly, but a large bruise spread like a blackberry stain. It was a pretty shade.

Some state his shanks were in now. He'd legged it fast enough, though. Shanks's pony had raced out of town at a gallop!

The damage to his chin he couldn't see. It would be the same purple colour, no doubt. What a sight he must look. A proper wounded soldier.

Next he checked over his pack. In the tussle with Jethro the buckle had loosened. Gwilym opened it up and laid out his possessions.

They were all there: the wooden plate and spoon made by Dada; woollen stockings made by Ma; spare flannel shirt and breeches from Mrs Davies; a tin with the left-over cheese from Mrs Williams; a knife with a worn blade but very sharp, kept in the tin with the cheese; a knife in a leather sheath given by Dafydd Williams; the comb from Hefin Williams; the brown and cream checked shawl which belonged to his mother. All present and correct.

He felt in his pocket for his water bottle. It was there. It hadn't fallen out in his wild rush to get away from Market Town.

But where was the money?

15

Where was the money from the sale of the things from his old home? He'd saved it all so far. The shilling from Mr Davies he could feel in the secret pocket in his waistcoat. The rest of the money had been in the drawstring purse tied around his waist. It hung on his left side.

Gwilym clutched at his side in panic. He could feel the string, but no purse. The string must have broken and the purse fallen when he struggled with Jethro.

Jethro must have picked it up! How he must be laughing! Anger and frustration swept over him. The money was to pay for lodgings when he reached Iron Town. To buy food; to help him survive until he found a job. He couldn't expect people to help him out all the time. 'You've got to pay your way in this world,' his Dada had told him.

How could he pay his way now? At least he'd save the cheese until he was really hungry. Until then he would eat more hazelnuts from the hedgerow. Hawthorn leaves too; they weren't called *bara menyn bara caws* for nothing. Other hungry lads must have sampled the green bread and cheese many times before him.

He bent forward to pick up his things. There was a lump at the small of his back. What was it? Jethro hadn't kicked him there. It didn't hurt. He was numb, that was it. That gallop had done for him. Gingerly he felt the lump through his shirt. His fingers touched the familiar bulge of the purse. It had twisted completely around his waist. Thankfully he scrabbled it back in place. Oh, the relief!

Anxiety had made his mouth dry and his tongue as rough as stone. Gwilym took the top off the water bottle and had a long drink. His tongue explored his mouth: his teeth felt as woolly as a sheep's fleece.

Guiltily he remembered that he had not cleaned his teeth since he began his journey. To do that he had to find a willow tree. His Ma had taught him to clean them with strips of willow. Dada had shown him where the trees could be found: near a river.

Gwilym trudged on until he heard the welcome sound of running water. He scrambled down a grassy bank, clinging to the branches of alder trees to stop him sliding. Cautiously he stood on the riverside rocks. First he stooped to fill his water bottle. Then he cupped his hands and sluiced water over his face. His skin tingled with the cold. Through eyelashes beaded with water drops he saw the willow trees. Their water-loving roots held them firmly to the river bank and their graceful branches leaned towards him, just within his reach.

Using his Dada's knife, he swiftly cut strips of willow and packed them into his food tin. He ate the cheese that was left, because he decided he was really hungry. It must be twelve o'clock he thought, remembering Dan-with-a-watch. Then, feeling virtuous, he rubbed a willow strip over and between his teeth.

Refreshed, he clambered back up to the roadway, in time to see a heavily laden cart come by. The heavy-hoofed carthorse tossed up its head, eyes wide and startled, and stopped in its tracks.

The carter, sitting high above, gave a growling shout, urging the animal on.

'You frightened Betsan, boy, coming out of the bushes like that,' he called down to Gwilym.

'Sorry. I didn't know you were near,' he answered, walking alongside Betsan and speaking softly to her. He didn't want to frighten horses as Jed had done.

'Going far?' asked the carter.

'Only to Iron Town,' said Gwilym airily.

'It's a fair step still to Iron Town,' said the carter.

'How long will it take me to cover a fair step?' asked Gwilym.

'Half the time if you care to climb on board,' said the carter. 'It's to Iron Town that I am going.'

16

Gwilym needed no second invitation. He heaved himself up beside the carter, almost losing his balance as the mare lurched forward in response to the reins slapped against her broad brown back. They were on their way. Hoof prints in the drying-out mud held puddles of water in their horseshoe shapes, showing the turnpike road was well-used.

Gwilym clung to the seat, unused to the swaying motion. He felt sick. Bumping over the rutted road made his stomach churn. The carter glanced at him.

'You're sitting too stiff, lad,' he said.

Gwilym relaxed his grip. The carter was right. It was easier to cope with the movement by swaying with it.

'So it's to Iron Town you're going, is it?' asked the carter, when he saw his passenger's face had regained its healthy pink.

Gwilym nodded. Not yet trusting himself to open his mouth.

'Another fresh-faced country lad to be fed into the hungry maw of Iron Town,' said the carter sadly.

'Don't like the way you put it,' said Gwilym.

'That's how it is, though,' said the carter.

'You work there! That's where you are going!' pointed out Gwilym.

'No, lad. I don't work there. I sell my potatoes there and then I'm off out of the place. After I've had a jar or two,' explained the carter. 'I remember when the town of Tydfil the Martyr was just a hamlet with farmers and sheep and whitewashed cottages, pretty against the green of the wooded hills. Since the iron trade came, the place has grown. Biggest town in Wales it is, with eight thousand people there now, so they say. The shame is, it attracts the biggest villains as well as honest workmen.'

'Why's that?'

'Workmen earn money. Come pay day there's money about. Where there's money there'll be thieves wanting to steal it.'

'I heard some people talking about that!' Gwilym blurted out.

The carter gave him a sharp look.

'Talking about what?' he asked.

'Money. That there's money to be had easy in Iron Town,' said Gwilym.

'Who would those people be then?' asked the carter. 'Where did you hear them talking?'

Who? Where? Too many questions.

'Can't remember,' said Gwilym unconvincingly. It was something he had better keep to himself for the moment. 'What does Iron Town look like?'

The carter was silent, punishing his passenger for not giving an honest answer to his last questions. Then he relented.

'In the night, like the mouth of Hell it is. You can see the glare of it for miles before you get there. The furnaces light up the sky.'

The last few miles had been a long slow drag uphill. At the top of the rise Betsan was reined in for a welcome halt. The carter waved his whip at the scene before him.

'There it is,' he said.

The town lay cradled among softly-rounded mountains. The moorland of the mountain tops sloped down to meet wooded hillsides through which ugly swathes had been cut.

'They've cut all those trees down!' said Gwilym.

'To make iron,' said the carter.

'Trees to make iron?' exclaimed Gwilym. Did the man think he was daft just because he was a country boy?

'Charcoal,' said the carter. 'Charcoal comes from slow-burning the wood in a special way. They used it to fire the furnaces. Then they found coal. Heated it in ovens to make coke. Now they use coke.'

The carter pointed his whip at a rockface in the distance above the town.

'That's one of the limestone quarries,' he said.

'Lime stones to make iron I suppose,' said Gwilym with a grin.

'Yes.'

Gwilym could see horses pulling what looked like wooden tubs on wheels along the base of the quarry.

'So it's stones in those tubs, is it?'

'Yes,' replied the carter. 'They're called drams or trams, not tubs. They run on iron tramways. Over there men are mining the coal,' he went on, pointing to another scar on the landscape. 'They get coal from the Patches, too,' he said. 'They've got to dig out ironstone as well.'

Ironstone! That made sense at last!

'To make iron?' said Gwilym, teasing the carter.

'Yes,' he answered. 'That's all the ingredients needed to make iron. And water.'

Water to make iron? Gwilym gave up trying to understand the mysteries of making iron. He doubted the carter was telling him the truth. He looked at the town itself.

Hundreds of houses, more houses than in the whole of Market Town, huddled close around huge buildings with gigantic chimney stacks.

'Furnaces,' said the carter. 'That's where all the limestone, ironstone and coke go. Into the furnaces.'

The tall chimneys challenged the grey clouds

overhead with their own belching billows of smoke. An east wind scurried the clouds towards them. With it came an acrid scent that caught in Gwilym's throat, and a distant menacing sound of metal pounding metal. A fiery glare lit up the clouds and spilled its flaming reflection onto the river that flowed towards the town. It was a fiercesome sight.

'Iron Town,' said the carter.

17

As the cart rattled its way downhill towards the town, Gwilym clutched the cart's sides to stop himself being pitched out. Betsan was pulled to a halt before a spiked barrier across the road.

'That's the turnpike,' explained the carter. 'We stop here.'

'Can't see that you could do anything else.'

A man came out from the round building by the side of the road. He greeted the carter and held out his hand for the money the carter gave him. Then he pulled the barrier aside and Betsan moved forward.

'Why did you have to pay that man?' asked Gwilym.

'People who use the road have to pay a tax, called a toll. The man was the tollhouse keeper. The money goes to pay for the road to be mended.'

Gwilym wondered how much of the money would find its way into the pockets of his road-mender friends.

Now they were in Iron Town itself. Low, grimy stone dwellings pressed close all around. Groups of young men lounged in doorways of taverns that stank of ale. There was a look of Jethro about some of them. Women in work-worn skirts and shawls called out to the carter, wanting to know what produce he was bringing.

Betsan was halted again, this time outside a hostelry.

'This is as far as I'll take you,' he told Gwilym. 'I'll be doing my trading from here.'

'That'll be thirsty work,' said Gwilym.

The carter laughed. 'Off with you! I wish you good luck in spite of your impudence.'

Gwilym slid from the cart, shrugged his shoulders to settle his pack more comfortably on his bones, thanked the carter, and set off. Threading his way through the streets, he tried to keep clear of the filth flung into the centre. People jostled into him, hardly noticing him. This was a different place from Market Town.

A hard place this was, like the iron it made.

His explorations led him along narrow streets and alleys, past ale house after ale house. Making iron must be even thirstier work than selling potatoes, he thought.

Curiosity led him into a bailey, a flagstoned courtyard with houses on all sides. It had only one way out, the way he had come in. A gang of boys was crouched down playing marbles. After the thumping he'd had in Market Town from Jethro, he was cautious about approaching them. But he was noticed. A scrawny boy in a ragged shirt saw him and shouted at him. The other boys looked up and began cat-calling and jeering.

Gwilym did not want to be caught in a place where he could be surrounded. He turned sharply and ran.

Turning a corner he stumbled against a woman carrying a pail of water. She screamed at him, cursing his clumsiness, as water slopped over her skirt.

'Hours I've waited for this bucketful of water and you've made me lose half of it, you bumpkin!'

Red-faced Gwilym stammered, 'Sorry!' and dodged a blow she aimed at his head. If the men and boys of Iron Town were a tough breed, the women were just as formidable, Gwilym decided.

Busy as a beehive, was Iron Town, and with many stings.

18

Gwilym had to ask many times: 'Where can I get lodgings?' Some people ignored him, brushing past as if he was just a shadow on the wall. Some men gave a shake of the head and hurried on. They had no time to waste on a lad seeking shelter.

It took Gwilym hours to roam the town. As he made his way down steps to yet another grim row of houses, his aching muscles began to rebel. Shanks's pony was tiring.

He sat on a windowsill to rest. An old man wearing a red muffler around his thin neck came slowly near and looked at him. It was a slight sign of interest, enough to prompt Gwilym to ask the question once more.

'Lodgings!' exclaimed the man. 'Every other house in Iron Town is a lodging house. The place is bursting at the seams.'

'Why?' asked Gwilym.

'I'll tell you. Where there's work, there's people needing work. Where there's people they need houses. Trouble is, with so many people flooding in to find work, there's not enough houses.'

Gwilym ventured another 'Why?'

'Can't be built fast enough, that's why. Thousands of people are in Iron Town now. Crowded, it is. So people who have houses rent out rooms. Ask around.'

As the old man walked away, Gwilym gathered up his pack to continue his search. A young woman, standing in a doorway, was idly watching passers-by. She wore a heavy grey skirt and a blouse that had once been white. Across her bosom was a checked shawl, something like the one that had been his mother's. He stopped and looked into her face. Hard eyes she had, not the motherly look he had perhaps hoped for.

'What are you lookin' at?' she said sharply.

'Nothing,' said Gwilym.

'Nothin', am I,' said the woman. 'There's cheek.'

'I'm looking *for* something, though,' said Gwilym.

'What then?' asked the woman.

'Lodgings. Only for the night.' Gwilym did not want to ask for too much.

'You'll be lucky!' the woman almost snorted. 'There's hardly room to move in this town. Lodgers everywhere. Night shift workers sleep in the beds in the day. Day shift workers sleep in the beds at night.'

'The same beds?' Gwilym was shocked.

'You've got money to pay for lodgings, have you?' the woman asked abruptly.

'For the night,' repeated Gwilym cautiously.

The woman gave a sideways jerk of her head.

'You can stay here.'

'How much?' asked Gwilym.

The woman told him.

'And breakfast,' bargained Gwilym.

'Let's see your money,' said the woman.

'When I've seen the room,' said Gwilym.

Turning, the woman led him through her kitchen, up a narrow stone stairway into a dark room with a number of beds in it. There were sleeping bodies in all but one of the beds already.

'Take that one over there,' said the landlady.

So Gwilym spent his first night in Iron Town in a lodging house.

He pulled up the blanket that smelled of other men's sweat and stared over the top of it into the raftered darkness of the roof. He remembered his own little home. That, too, was crowded, but he'd had his own dear Ma and Dada and little brother and sister around him there. Here he was in the company of strangers who did not even know his name.

He turned over. Putting his fingers in his ears to muffle the snoring and troubled dream sounds from the other lodgers, he at last relaxed into the silence of sleep.

19

A rough hand shook him awake. Gwilym blinked in the grey light of early morning seeping through the grimy window. A man with tired eyes and bristled chin stood beside the bed.

'Out of there, lad,' he said. 'I need my sleep now.'

Gwilym slid reluctantly from beneath the blanket, feeling his warm toes touch the chill of the bare floorboards. Gathering his belongings hanging from a wooden peg on the wall, he pulled on his breeches and stockings, pushed his feet into his boots and clattered downstairs, his shirt-tail flapping loose.

The landlady stooped over the coal fire, stirring a cooking pot. She turned to see him hesitating in the doorway, his shirt still undone.

'There's no water for you to wash, so do your shirt up,' she said abruptly. 'The men used up all the spare water I collected yesterday.'

Gwilym didn't care; he just buttoned up his shirt and tucked it into his breeches.

'Fetch me that bowl,' she ordered.

Gwilym brought the bowl from the table and held it out for her. Two heaped spoonfuls of cooked oatmeal were tapped sharply against the bowl to dislodge their sticky load. Using the spoon his Dada had made, he ate the scalding porridge. It slithered hot down his gullet to fill the hungry hollow in his belly.

Shadowy figures went in procession past the window. Nailed boots scraped the cobblestones. Workers were on their way to quarries, mines, foundry and furnace. If he joined them he could surely find work for himself. He blew cooling breath on the porridge so that he could eat faster and join the men before they disappeared. Licking his spoon clean, he pocketed it, and turned his back on the landlady to fish out the money he owed. She took the money without a word. He thanked her for the porridge, picked up his pack and stepped out into the morning frost.

There was no doubt Iron Town was an exciting place and he had not yet seen its fiery heart. He remembered one of his mother's sayings, 'When the days lengthen the cold strengthens.' He'd get a job in the Iron Works. It would be warm there, at least.

Boldly he stepped in front of a hurrying workman.

'Where's the iron works, mister?' he asked.

'Which one? There's four in Iron Town now,' was the unexpected answer.

'The nearest one then,' said Gwilym.

The man was amused. 'That's where I'm going.'

'I'll come with you,' said Gwilym.

'Will you indeed,' said the man and walked away.

Gwilym tagged along behind. He followed the man into a street with taller houses, behind which rose a steep-sided hill. The road curved and soon led into a workyard.

Never could Gwilym have imagined such activity, such a deafening racket. On the right was a long stone building with six arched entrances. Ahead was a sturdy iron bridge spanning the river he had seen from a distance the day before. As he turned left he saw a group of giant buildings with steeply sloping roofs from which protruded the chimneys he had seen.

High up at the far end of the yard, a channel made of wood and iron spilled water over the top and into the troughs of a giant waterwheel. The wheel revolved ponderously, in rhythm with the weight of water, as the troughs filled and sank, to what purpose Gwilym could not tell.

The workman he had shadowed beckoned him to stand beside him in front of a high arched entrance.

'They cook rocks in there,' he said. 'Watch this. They're going to tap the furnace.'

Gwilym peered into the cavernous hall and glimpsed the black shape of a furnace-man thrusting a long rod into the side of a mysterious square edifice. White hot molten metal spewed out, showering sparks of orange and gold in a display of awesome beauty.

'That's iron,' said the workman with quiet pride.

The liquid iron was running into a strangely shaped trench in the deep sand on the floor.

'That's the sow and her piglets,' said the workman.

Sow and piglets! It was nothing like them. Gwilym had seen a sow with piglets busy sucking at her teats.

This glowing iron trench was more like a leaf worn away to its veins, thick straight ones: unyielding metal bars.

'Pig iron it's called,' said the workman. 'When the iron cools they break the piglets away from the sow, so there's two sizes of metal bars to work with, or to sell. Watch this again, boy. He's going to knock out one more clay plug.'

A second thrust into the side of the furnace brought forth yet another molten mass that spread fire, spitting as it cooled, over the sanded floor.

'That's slag. Useless that is,' said the workman. 'Seen anything like this before, lad?'

Gwilym, blasted by heat, eyes dry as grit, shook his head.

'Vulcans, these men are,' said the workman. 'Gods of furnace and foundry. There's been nothing like this since the world began.'

He turned away and pointed. 'Over there is the foundry and the workshops.'

The noise from the workshops was loud. The man was not shouting, yet Gwilym could understand almost every word he uttered. He mouthed the words, not attempting to compete with the noise that enveloped them. Disheartened, Gwilym thought, how could I work in a place like this? He know nothing that could be of any use to the iron men in this place of heat and noise and danger.

Then, across the yard came the rumble of a journey of trams. A team of horses hauled the trams over tracks which snaked over the yard. Calmly, amidst the industrial clamour, the horses plodded on about their task.

Horses! Where there were horses Gwilym might yet find work.

20

'Where do I go to ask for a job with horses?' Gwilym asked the workman. He pointed the way.

'There's the farrier's place over by the stables,' he said. 'Tell him I sent you,' he added kindly.

Gwilym stepped carefully over the tramrails that criss-crossed the yard and looked into the farrier's workplace. A small wiry man wearing a leather apron over his clothes grunted a question. Gwilym did not hear what it was so answered what he thought it might have been.

'I've been sent here. I'm looking for a JOB with HORSES!' he shouted.

'Who sent you?' the farrier mouthed.

'Him, that man.' Gwilym waved his hand vaguely in the direction of where the workman had been.

'Well he's not there now,' said the farrier.

Gwilym looked around. The man indeed was not there and had, no doubt, gone about his own business.

'What was his name?' asked the farrier.

'Don't know,' said Gwilym.

'So you've been sent to look for a job by a man whose name you don't know and who isn't even there.' Gwilym felt foolish. 'Some recommendation that is,' grumbled the farrier. 'Think I'm daft, do you?'

'No sir. I'm the daft one,' replied Gwilym.

'We can agree on that,' said the farrier. 'In from the country are you?'

'Yes. How did you know?'

'From the fresh look about you. I'm sorry to disappoint you, lad, but I've no work for you. But keep trying and be careful. You seem to be a decent lad and there are some places and people around here you should be wary of.'

'Why?' asked Gwilym, interested.

'Thieves and robbers, lad. They prey on honest workers. Where there's pay in pockets there'll be men and boys, and, sad to say, women and girls, who'll pick 'em.'

Gwilym thought of the purse tied around his waist. *He* wouldn't get his pocket picked.

As he turned to leave, the farrier called out to him.

'Try here again in a week's time.'

'What day is it today?' asked Gwilym.

'Tuesday,' answered the farrier. 'Why?'

'So's I'll know when seven days are up. See you next Tuesday Mr er . . .'

'Evans,' responded the farrier. 'Charlie Evans.'

Gwilym left the noise and bustle of the yard, pondering how to work out when the week was over. He'd get a stick, make a notch in it every night. When he had seven notches in the stick, the next day would be Tuesday. He was glad his Ma had taught

73

him the names of the seven days in a week. Hope of a job, even if in seven long days' time, put confidence in Gwilym. His next task was to find a piece of stick.

It had been raining again. Hearing the sound of a fast flowing river, he went in search of it. There'd surely be trees growing on the river bank as there had been when he'd needed to cut the strips of willow to clean his teeth.

He came to a bridge. Leaning far over the stone parapet, he was fascinated by the swift rush of water below. It made him dizzy, and disappointed.

There were no trees. The river, pure and clear as it might once have been, was now black, its banks covered in filth and debris, where only a few brave weeds struggled to grow.

'Never seen a river before?' said a jeering voice.

Gwilym turned around. A crowd of boys had gathered. They were the boys from the bailey. Their clothes were ragged. The jeering one had on a wide-brimmed hat.

'I've seen cleaner rivers,' said Gwilym.

'Cleaner ones, eh? Are you saying that Iron Town's river, our river, is dirty?' mocked Big Hat.

'It's not clean,' said Gwilym.

'He's rude about our river!'

'Chuck 'im in!'

'Up with 'im!'

The boys seized Gwilym by his jacket and pulled him roughly about.

'Let go!' he yelled.

'Shall we chuck 'im in, or make him pay for insulting our river?' Big Hat shouted.

'Make 'im pay! Make 'im pay!'

Two of the boys were tugging at his pack. Gwilym flailed his arms and kicked. One kick caught Big Hat on the shin. He yelled in pain.

'Scrag 'im!'

It was a command.

Gwilym screwed up his eyes as fists punched his face and body. Blindly, he fought off his attackers. But they were too many for him. They brought him to the ground. As he fell he tasted blood, his own blood.

21

Gwilym lay still. Kicks and thumps rammed into his body. Curled up, his knees drawn up to his chin, he protected his head with his arms.

It's like a hedgehog I am, he thought. Through his pain he remembered a spiny creature he had once tormented and felt sorry for what he had done.

The gang tugged at his clothes, dragged off his pack and with triumphant whoops, ran away.

Cautiously he uncurled himself and scrambled to his feet. He looked for his pack but it had gone. Anger burned in him.

The boys had picked a good time for their assault, for it was a rare moment in that crowded town: the street was empty. Everybody else was at work, he assumed.

His shirt had been pulled up out of his breeches. As he tucked it back in place he clutched his waist. The precious purse had been taken. Only the now useless cord remained. It had been cut. He drew it out, gazing at it blankly. He felt in the secret pocket of his waistcoat. It was empty of his precious silver coin.

Why had he ever come to Iron Town? While he had money to pay his way he had hope. Now he was penniless.

Blood tasted like salt in his mouth and with his tongue he explored the source. His lip was cut and felt swollen. The shock of what had happened left him numb. He no longer knew what to do.

A gentle rain still fell. At first he barely noticed it. The day had darkened, or as dark as it could get in Iron Town, surrounded as it was with glowing slag tips and the glare of the furnaces.

Shift workers were hurrying home. As before, no-one noticed him, damp, dishevelled and blood-stained as he was. The rain penetrated his jacket and dripped from his hair. Now he knew what to do. He looked around for shelter. Under the bridge. That was the nearest place.

He went to the end of the bridge, climbed over the parapet and dropped down. The river bank was slippery. He slithered through the mud towards the arch of the bridge.

The black river, whose speeding sound had first

drawn him to it, flowed unheedingly past. Gwilym found a dry place, sat with his arms around his knees, rested his head on his arms, and allowed himself to sink into despair.

Cold, friendless, alone. He wept.

22

As the winter sun rose the following morning it sparkled weakly on the river flowing towards the bridge. It had no warmth to give the forlorn figure still resting under the shadowed arch. It was its light which roused the boy.

Gwilym was cold. So cold that it hurt and his arms and legs were ice. He shivered, teeth chattering. Stiffly he struggled upright. Stamping his feet, he flung his arms repeatedly around his body. In a while, warming blood began to throb painfully in his fingers and toes.

Then he clambered up the river bank back to street level. People hurried by. Now he felt even more insignificant. Yesterday he had some money, some belongings to remind him of his home and friends. Today he had nothing but the clothes he stood in. He wandered on. The rain had stopped and the clothes were drying on his back.

Gwilym came across a coaching inn, its sign swinging and a wide archway leading to its inner courtyard. It was the kind where stage coaches called to pick up passengers, parcels and letters. Gwilym had not come across it before. He lingered, hopeful for scraps to fill his rumbling belly.

A well-dressed gentleman in a dark blue full-skirted coat rode up, slid from the saddle, flung the reins in Gwilym's direction with the instruction, 'Hold my horse, lad,' and strode into the inn.

Gladly Gwilym held the reins, stroking the horse's gleaming chestnut coat, happy to share its warmth. Here was a well cared-for animal.

When the man returned with the stink of ale on his breath he remounted, flung down a copper penny in payment and rode off. Here was a way to make a few pence. Gwilym stooped to pick it up. It bore the sideways view of a fat-faced man with leaves wrapped around his head.

A clatter of shifting hooves came from the inner yard. Gwilym ventured under the archway and found more horses tethered there. He stood between them, talking softly and stroking them. One mare shifted uneasily away from him. Her flanks had been raked raw by spurs.

There was something about the animal that was familiar. The droop of her neck reminded him of the other sad mare in the stable of the White Rock Tavern. Could this be Jed's mare? If it was, he must be up to no good here.

The back door of the inn was open. Inside, a mob-capped woman was busy with steaming pots on a huge open fire. A red-faced man wearing a blood-stained apron was cutting up the carcass of a sheep.

By the look of it the knife must have been very sharp for it was slicing through the meat as if through water.

He went to the front of the inn again and leaned against the wall near the window, waiting for more horsemen to ride up and throw him pennies.

Voices raised in argument came through the window, which was partly open at the top. Looking through the window, Gwilym saw there were only three men in the room. They sat at a settle by the fire with pint pots in their hands. Two of the men, one with a bulging belly, the other weasel-faced, were doing most of the talking. They were responding to an occasional question from the third man.

The third man's face was in shadow. His booted legs moved and firelight gleamed on cruel spurs. The kind that could draw blood.

The man in the shadows was Jed, who had said there was money for the taking in Iron Town. Well, Gwilym's money had already been taken.

Who would Jed steal from? Thieves stole from workers, the carter had told him. Gwilym had seen how furnace men sweated at their work. Honest sweat. The thought of those men being cheated of their hard-earned pay made Gwilym angry.

If he could find out what Jed was up to, perhaps he could earn a reward. That would put honest money back in his own pocket. As Jed had never seen him, Gwilym felt it was safe enough to loiter. He might discover what he was planning.

Pretending to look idly around from his listening

post, Gwilym tried to catch the conversation going on inside.

The fat-bellied man's voice was boastful. Jed interrupted with a quiet question. The Fat Man was silent, but there was the sound of a pint pot being set down.

Jed raised his voice. 'More ale! Innkeeper! More ale! There's men in here with a great thirst and I've dust to settle in my throat from my journey.'

'Wait a moment! We're short-handed here!' came an irritated cry from the kitchen.

Gwilym shot around to the back door again. Here was a chance worth taking. Boldly he entered the kitchen.

'Hey! What do you think you are doing?' shouted the man in the bloodied apron who must have been the innkeeper.

'I can help,' said Gwilym. 'I can carry things,' he added hopefully.

'You're not fit to be seen in company,' said the innkeeper. 'Get out!'

'Don't be so hard-hearted, Llew,' said the woman. 'I could do with help, what with Ceinwen not being here. What can you do, lad?' she asked.

'Peel potatoes,' said Gwilym, glad of the lesson he'd had from Mrs Williams at Cefn Glas.

Mrs Llew turned to her husband. 'That'll do. He'll be a big help this morning. And he can be pot boy.'

'He'll have to clean himself up,' said Llew.

Gwilym was given a brush to get rid of the dried mud on his clothes and told to wash at the pump in the yard. It was one of the few places in the town which had its own spring water.

'Ale! Where's that ale?' Jed's impatience sharpened his voice.

'Fetch their pots, boy,' ordered Llew.

Gwilym hurried to do his bidding. Llew filled the pint pots to the brim with foaming ale and set them on a tray. Gwilym carried the tray carefully so as not to spill the drinks and put them on the table in front of the customers.

Hands reached out for them, a fat greedy hand, a thin bony hand, a gloved rider's hand. Gwilym took the tray away, went quietly behind the settle, pretended to wipe the tray with his sleeve, and listened.

Fat Man was describing a horse. Black, he said it was, with a white blaze and two white legs, right foreleg, left hind leg.

'Fridays,' said the Fat Man, answering another question from Jed.

'Always?' It was Jed's query again.

'Always. Like clockwork. You'll have to make your own arrangements as to new horseflesh. I cannot. It might draw suspicion on me.'

Weasel Face sniggered. 'It would have to be a carthorse to carry your weight, John, and that would not be fleet enough for Mr Jed's purpose.'

'It can't be done this Friday, then,' said Jed thoughtfully.

Jed was getting information from the men, and he was paying for it, for the moment, in ale. Information about what? It had to be something to do with thievery. Gold? Money? From what he had seen so far, Iron Town was a hard-working place but not a rich one. Then he recalled the carter's words '. . . Where there's work there's money in men's pockets . . .'

Could Jed be going around picking pockets, attacking people just as Gwilym himself had been attacked? He could not imagine Jed having the stomach to attack any ironman. There had to be something else he had in mind.

'Boy!' Mrs Llew's irate voice came from the kitchen. 'Come and do the potatoes!'

Gwilym had few chances to go back to overhear what Jed was up to, for he was up to his knees in potatoes. He had never seen so many of the knobbly brown things. By the end of the day his fingers were sore, but Mrs Llew had fed him well on *cawl* and bread.

He had hoped that Mrs Llew would ask him to come back the next day, but what she said was, 'We won't be needing you tomorrow for Ceinwen will be here.'

But she paid him for his work and gave him ale to drink before he left the inn. Jed's mare was no longer tethered outside.

The ale made his head feel it was floating away from his shoulders. In a bemused state he drifted around the town.

Suddenly he saw a familiar checked shawl, his mother's shawl! His mind cleared. He raced after the figure wearing the shawl, dodging around people to keep the woman in sight. She turned to go down a narrow lane and was about to step into her house when a breathless Gwilym caught up with her.

'The shawl!' he gasped. 'It's my Ma's shawl!'

The woman, startled, spun around.

'Are you accusing me of stealing?' she snapped.

'No! No! It was stolen from me by a gang of boys.'

The woman clutched the shawl closer to her shoulders.

'I bought this,' she said. 'Paid good money for it, I tell you.'

'Did you buy it from a boy in a big hat?'

'Yes,' she agreed.

'His gang set on me and stole everything I had,' explained Gwilym.

The woman's face softened. Gwilym noticed the change.

'I'm an orphan,' he added with calculating melancholy.

Her face became hard. 'Oh yes,' she said disbelievingly. 'I know what you're up to. You're in the gang yourself, I'm sure. The other boy gets the money selling the shawl; you run after me with this story of yours thinking I'll give it to you out of the goodness of my heart, you take it back to the gang and sell it again! Think I'm daft, do you? Well, think again, because I'm not parting with it,' and she slammed the door.

Gwilym was stunned. To be accused of stealing his own mother's shawl was so unfair. To be accused of belonging to Big Hat's gang was insulting. This was another sting Iron Town had inflicted. There was worse to come.

Iron Town's night was drawing in. The money he had earned that day was not enough to buy him lodging. In any case he wanted to save it to buy food.

It was not raining. He'd find a quiet corner to curl up in somewhere.

What he found was a cinder pile. A comforting warmth came from coal fragments smouldering deep inside. This was the place for him.

He lay down, wriggling his body into place, as he had done in the straw in Cefn Glas cowshed. Relaxed, he happily disregarded the fumes gently rising from the tip's still dangerously burning interior.

Unnoticed, on the other side of the tip, a stray dog, tempted by the same lethal warmth, had also curled up to sleep.

It was already dead.

23

Someone was shaking him by the shoulders. A voice was shouting at him. 'Wake up! Wake up!' Back in bed in the lodging house, was he? He was warm, very warm. He did not want to get up. He just wanted to lie there, warm, comfortable and still.

The shouting went on, louder, more urgent. He was being shaken until his teeth rattled. His mouth and nose were filled with a strange taste and scent.

Sleepily, with difficulty, he opened his eyes. It was

84

still dark but the moon slid from behind a cloud and lit up the face of the man who was shaking him.

It was the most terrifying face he had ever seen. Gwilym's startled eyes told of his fear. The man dropped his hands.

'You're still alive then, but you won't last much longer if you stay on these cinders. The fumes will kill you. Didn't anyone tell you how dangerous these tips are? Get off! Now!'

Gwilym scrambled off the rustling cinders, dusty and frightened.

'No-one told me,' he said.

'You're new here,' said the man.

'Yes,' said Gwilym, not looking at him.

'Don't let my physog scare you, boy. There's men with handsome physogs and there's people like me you don't want to look at twice, but villains can have pretty faces and people like me can be as good as any angel in Heaven,' said the man.

'Don't see any wings on you,' said Gwilym.

The man chuckled. 'You've got spirit, boy. What's your name? Where've you come from?'

Gwilym told him his story.

'I've lost everything. I suppose if it wasn't for you I'd have lost my life as well.'

'Iron Town is a hard place for grown men and women. It's harder on children and young 'uns,' said the man. 'How do you feel now? You look groggy enough. Try and walk about a bit. We mustn't hang around here or I'll be keeling over as well.'

They walked the streets together slowly, for

Gwilym to recover from the effects of the fumes. He glanced at the man quickly, curious to see if his face was as frightful as it first appeared. The man sensed his interest.

'It helps if you look at my left eye first,' he said quietly.

Emboldened, Gwilym stopped and looked the man fully in the face. The left eye was grey, with a thick black eyebrow, and smile wrinkles around. It was a shrewd eye. A friendly eye.

But the right half of the man's face was wrecked. The flesh of his cheek was puckered as though stitched together, pulling up one side of his mouth into a mirthless grin. The same rough stitchery had drawn his right eyelid down into a sinister wink. The eyebrow was cleft in two. Pink new skin was growing over the red rawness of the wounds. So delicate was the skin that Gwilym felt that if he touched it, even ever so gently, it would melt, like thin ice, under the warmth of his finger.

Gwilym gazed in open wonder at the ruin of the man's face.

'What happened?' he asked bluntly.

'A kiss from the blast furnace, lad. My Lady Furnace blew me a kiss so I'd always remember the encounter.'

Gwilym was confused.

'Molten iron,' explained the man. 'You can't always predict My Lady's change of mood. She gave me a face that has the masks of both tragedy and comedy on it.'

'How did you mend it?' asked Gwilym.

'Mend it? The wounds, you mean? A friend of mine mended it as you say. Gifted in the art of healing wounds is Frederick the Great.'

Gwilym's aching head began to reel.

'My head . . . giddy . . .' he managed to mutter, and sank to the ground.

24

Cool water trickled over his face. The terrible taste that had been in his mouth since sleeping on the cinder tip seemed to have lessened. His head still ached, but otherwise he was comfortable. Too comfortable. This was dangerous. He would have to get up.

Gwilym struggled to rise.

'Mus . . . gerrup . . . don . . . wan . . . wake . . . up dead,' he muttered.

'Think you're still on the cinder heap, do you?' said a deep voice. 'Lie back: you're safe enough here.'

Where was here? A gentle hand was wiping away the reviving water. Gwilym opened his eyes fully. He was lying in a box bed in a whitewashed kitchen. Bunches of herbs hung from the ceiling. The room smelled sweetly clean. He took a deep breath. The taste of cinder fumes that had clogged his throat had almost gone.

He was better, much better, but not enough to get out of bed just yet.

He turned his head, expecting to see his new friend, the man-kissed-by-the-furnace. But it was an older man, with battered ears and a bony face as craggy as a quarry, who sat beside the bed, squeezing out the cloth with which he had been wiping Gwilym's forehead.

'Fred, I am,' he said. 'Ianto carried you here. Feel better, do you?'

Gwilym nodded.

'Haven't had much of a welcome in Iron Town then,' said Fred.

Gwilym nodded.

'Hungry, lad?'

Gwilym nodded.

This was good. He was being offered food as well as having his face washed.

Fred scraped back his chair and went over the flagstoned floor to the cauldron set over the fire in the hearth. He ladled some of its contents into a bowl and brought it back to Gwilym.

Gwilym sat up and accepted the offering.

'Rabbit stew, this is,' said Fred.

'Where's Ianto then?' Gwilym asked after he had eaten.

'Rabbiting,' said Fred.

As he himself told Gwilym later, Ianto had been doing more than catching wild rabbits. After he set the snares to catch rabbits on the mountain that rose behind Fred's furze-thatched cottage, he had gone in search of Big Hat and his gang.

From Gwilym's description of the boys and the place where he had first seen them, Ianto knew the bailey where they usually gathered to share the spoils of their thieving excursions around the streets.

Patiently Ianto had waited until the gang came gleefully racing back from their latest venture.

'They stopped laughing when they saw me,' he told Gwilym later, as he related what had happened.

'I told them, "You've got things belonging to a friend of mine," and I listed all the items they'd stolen. The boy you called Big Hat is Billy Davies; do you know what he said then? He said, "They're ours now." Defiant he was, but I told him he didn't get them by fair means. "You set on him, a lone lad new to Iron Town, with the whole of your gang. Too afraid to tackle him on your own it seems," that's what I told him and he didn't like it. "No, I'm not," he said. Quite indignant he was. "I'll fight What's-'is-name any time, any where." "You heard that, boys," I said to the rest of the gang. "I said, if the lad wins, you'll have to give back all you've stolen from him."

'Billy was grinning. He liked a fight, he said. Cheeky he was. Wanted to know what he'd get when he won. Said he wasn't going to fight just for stuff he's already got. I said there'll be a winner's purse,' said Ianto. 'That was a bit reckless of me, I'll worry about where to get the money later. But I made Billy agree that you'll have your belongings back. We slapped hands on it.'

'Me? Fight Billy Big Hat?' Gwilym was horrified.

'Why should I fight for something that's mine anyway?'

'It's the only way you'll get any of it back. Billy's said he'll fight you for it and said it in front of his gang. He'll have to stick to his word or lose their respect, and respect for his bullying ways is what keeps him head of the gang,' explained Ianto.

'It's you who challenged him to fight me, without asking me, mind,' said Gwilym indignantly, 'and there's just one other thing,' he added, 'I won't fight.'

'Won't fight?' Ianto was quite shocked.

'I can scrap a bit but I've never been in a proper fight,' said Gwilym. ' And Billy's not the type who'll fight fair.'

'Fred and me'll teach you. He's not called Frederick the Great for nothing. He was the best bare knuckle mountain fighter in the Valley.'

'When?' asked Gwilym suspiciously, looking at Fred's grey hair.

'Oh, about fifteen years ago,' said Ianto.

'Don't worry, Gwilym, I may be grey-headed but I haven't forgotten the tricks of the trade,' said Fred, standing up, his arms loose at his sides but his hands already clenched into fists.

According to the terms Ianto had arranged, the reluctant Gwilym had some days to prepare for the fight.

'We agreed that first to be downed three times loses the fight,' explained Ianto to an increasingly gloomy Gwilym.

Some friend Ianto had turned out to be.

25

Frederick the Great, gentle though he was in spirit, was hard as iron itself in body.

'We'll have to toughen you up, Gwilym,' he said.

First he took Gwilym to the mountain stream near the cottage and made him hold his fists in the icy rushing water until they were red raw with cold. Then he rubbed vinegar into them. After that he slathered goose grease on Gwilym's arms and pummelled their muscles. All the while he poured out his fund of knowledge about boxing.

'Balance,' he said. 'You must keep your balance. Legs apart for better balance. Remember that.

'Keep moving,' he said. 'Stand still and you'll be done for.

'Fists up,' he said. 'Right fist up to protect your chin, left fist out to keep t'other lad at a distance.

'Eyes,' he said. 'Keep your eyes on those fists of his.'

After all that, Fred took Gwilym to a level patch of ground and made him go through the motions of a fight.

'Go on! Slam your fists into my hand,' he ordered. 'Harder, boy, harder! Your punch has as much clout as a battling bedbug!'

More insults were heaped on Gwilym's head, until Gwilym got mad and lunged wildly, flinging punches in all directions, fetching up punching Frederick the Great's belly. Filled with rock it was.

Fred laughed and held off the puny attack. He

tapped his student lightly on the side of the head, just enough to make it sting.

'The fighter who loses his temper loses the fight,' he said. 'Now try again. Don't let my words put you off. And this time put weight into your punches. Punch well into the body.'

So it went on. Endlessly it seemed. There was one compensation. Between the bouts of trying to fight Fred, Gwilym was fed, well fed. And he slept well and comfortably. Almost without noticing it happening, he had become part of Fred's household.

All thoughts of getting a job with Charlie Evans the farrier were pushed to the back of his mind. All thoughts at the front of his mind were dominated by preparations for The Fight.

By the morning of the day chosen for the fight Gwilym felt confident that he had absorbed all Fred's advice. He was fit, his muscles, such as they were, supple. He remembered the rough-and-tumble play fights he used to enjoy back home. But this was serious. He was fighting for all he had in the world.

26

A level patch of grass, close-cropped by sheep, was the agreed place for the fight. The day was bright with sun. Gwilym and his two mentors waited for Billy Big Hat and his gang to arrive. They waited half an hour, timed by an impressive watch Frederick the Great had won in a prize fight. It was by that watch he had taught Gwilym how to tell the time. Minutes dragged by. Gwilym's stomach was churning.

'I'm going to be sick,' he said.

'No you won't,' said Fred. 'Take deep breaths.'

Gwilym breathed deeply.

'Perhaps he won't come,' he suggested hopefully.

He was wrong.

Billy and eight faithful followers swaggered up the narrow sheep-track that led to the fight venue.

'You're late,' said Ianto.

'No timepiece,' said Billy. 'Had to ask.'

'It's a wonder you hadn't stolen one,' said Gwilym sourly.

'That's enough,' interrupted Fred. 'Now these are the rules for this fight . . .'

They were simple. No kicking, no hair pulling, no putting thumbs in eyes, or up noses, no punching below the breeches' belt.

'All for your safety, lads,' said Fred. 'First to be knocked down three times is the loser,' he added.

'What's the winner's purse then?' asked Billy, removing his big hat and giving it to his henchman Guto, a freckled boy with only two fingers on his right hand.

Ianto looked at Fred. They had both forgotten about the promised purse with its promise of money inside it.

'You sold my mother's shawl,' accused Gwilym. 'Even if I win the fight I won't be getting my Ma's shawl off you, so why should you expect a purse.

You've already got mine, and spent the money in it, I expect. I'm fighting to get back what you stole from me, not for any extra purse money. Don't see why you should be rewarded for thievery!' Gwilym was furious.

'You're right, boy,' agreed Ianto.

Unexpectedly Billy pulled from his pocket a familiar drawstring leather pouch, Gwilym's purse, and held it up.

'Here's your purse,' he announced. 'It's as heavy as when I took it from you. This is the purse I'll fight you for.'

Ianto was surprised. Was there an unexpected hint of chivalry in Billy's attitude?

'Let me keep the purse until after the fight,' he suggested. 'If Gwilym wins you might scarper off with it.'

'Don't you trust me?' sneered Billy.

'No,' said Ianto.

'That makes two of us,' said Billy. 'I don't trust you.'

'Then leave it on that stone over there, away from everybody until after the fight,' ordered Fred.

Billy Big Hat did as he was told, much to his own surprise. The leather pouch sat plumply on the flat stone, its drawstring tight, holding the contents safe. Gwilym was glad to see it again.

'Now then, on with the fight,' said Fred, taking command.

The two boys took off their coats and rolled up their shirt sleeves. In Billy's case there was not much of a ragged sleeve to roll.

Fred, Ianto and the rest of Billy's gang gathered round. Within the circle they created, the two young pugilists, fists up, moved cautiously around each other.

Gwilym's heart thumped, his eyes on Billy. All Fred's advice fled from his brain. His mind was blank.

Billy's grubby fist shot out and landed on Gwilym's nose. The gang roared their delight. The pain of the blow caused Gwilym to stagger back. Fred's voice rose above the racket.

'Remember what I taught you!'

Keep moving . . . keep your balance . . . keep your eyes on his fists . . . put weight into your punches . . .

Put weight into my punches! Haven't had a chance to land one yet . . . wish he'd stand still a minute . . .

'Ouch!' another blow landed and Gwilym, off-balance, fell.

Billy's triumphant grin curved up like a sickle blade. Standing over Gwilym, he joined with his gang in shouting insults.

This was too much. Gwilym scrambled to his feet. His clouded mind cleared. He danced around on his toes, shot out a punch which landed square on Billy's self-satisfied sneer. Then he moved lightly, rapidly . . . backwards. Billy chased him, flailing punches. Gwilym dodged. Billy, red-faced with effort, looked angrier by the second. Good, thought Gwilym, he's losing his temper.

Gwilym's right fist stayed close to his chin, his left fist parried the blows Billy was throwing. He saw a chance and let fly with his right fist, putting his shoulder into the weight of the punch. Billy fell.

A shocked silence was broken only by the sound of both boys' heavy breathing.

Billy was quickly up on his feet. The sneering look had left his face. Gwilym knew that from then on the fight was going to be tougher.

Gwilym dodged nimbly around with Billy, heavy-footed, windmilling his arms. Gwilym took more punches on his body, watching for a moment of carelessness that Billy was sure to show. It came. Gwilym's fist shot out. A surprised Billy fell again.

This time noise erupted.

'Get up, Billy!' Guto was yelling.

'Knock 'im out, Billy!' the boys were shouting.

Billy got to his feet quickly enough, but Gwilym could see he was tiring, his bare knuckles bruised and smothered in blood.

Gwilym spared a moment to wonder 'Is that my blood or his?'

Now his concentration was absolute. He had never felt sharper, more alive. He made Billy lumber after him. In despair Billy let out a kick to Gwilym's shin.

Fred's voice roared.

'One more like that and you're disqualified!'

Once more the boxers circled each other. Now Gwilym was tiring. It was time to try out one of the tricks of Fred's tough trade.

With his left arm held out, his right fist protecting his face, Gwilym made a feint with his left, Billy evaded and swiped forward. Gwilym moved sideways, dodged the blow and landed his right fist squarely on Billy's chin.

Down onto the trampled turf went Billy Big Hat.

First to be downed three times loses the match. That was the rule.

Breathing hard, Gwilym let his fists fall to his sides.

27

Gwilym was jubilant. He had downed Billy the Bully. He looked down on him, sprawled on the sweet green grass. Blood dripped from Billy's nose and a large purple bruise extended across his jaw.

Fred clapped Gwilym on the shoulder.

'Thought you'd lost it there for a bit, me lad,' he said. 'But you rallied. You did well for a learner.'

Then Fred held out his hardened hand to help Billy to his feet. As he did so Gwilym noticed for the first time how thin and pale the boy was. He looked around at Billy's gang. Subdued by their leader's defeat, downed by an out-of-town country lad, they were silent, sullen. Guto's damaged hand held Billy's over-sized hat. How did he come to lose his fingers? Maimed somewhere in Iron Town probably, as Gwilym's friend Ianto had been burned by the furnace. Maimed, burned. He remembered Siôn Williams's warning.

Back on his feet, Billy had his face wiped over with kindly Fred's dampened towel and walked over to the stone where Gwilym's drawstring purse lay. Picking it up he walked back to Gwilym. To Gwilym's astonishment Billy made a low bow, right foot forward, sweeping his arm across his body in a mocking version of a gentleman's greeting.

'The winner's purse!' he proclaimed, making a ceremony of it, holding it out for Gwilym to take.

Gwilym accepted the proffered purse. Not knowing how to cope with Billy's over-acting, he could only mumble an embarrassed 'Ta.'

Then, louder, he demanded, 'What about the rest of my belongings?'

'Let 'im have them, lads,' said Billy to the gang.

The boys delved into their poachers' hidden pockets and came forward with Gwilym's Dada's bowl and spoon, the Williams' comb and knife, the water bottle and the food tin. His spare clothes were already on the backs of some of the boys. There was no sign of them being given back. What he especially wanted was his Ma's shawl and he knew where that was.

Turning to Billy, Fred said, 'With a bit of training and building up I could make you into a passable pugilist.'

'Make a living being bashed about for men to make bets on? No thanks, grand-dad!' and, flinging his coat casually over his shoulder, Billy sauntered away, his gang falling in line behind him.

'Fair play, there's something of a leader about him,' said Ianto.

Gwilym scowled.

He did not like his friend praising his enemy, though he had to admit Billy had played fair, giving his purse back.

The purse was as heavy as it was before, so no money had been spent. He pulled open the drawstring.

Wordlessly he showed the contents to Ianto and Fred.

'Oh!' said Ianto.

Fred rubbed his battered hand over his grey hair. He said nothing.

Billy had filled the purse with stones. The fight had indeed been for a purse. One empty of money.

28

'Ianto: tell me, if Billy Davies had beaten me, what would he have won?' It was a fair question. Ianto carefully thought for an answer.

'I'd have given him my week's wages,' said Ianto. 'But he'd have had to wait for pay day to have it.'

The three friends had returned to Frederick the Great's cottage and were enjoying a meal of vegetable soup and bread. Gwilym was happy. But he was soon in for a disappointment. Fred waited until they had all eaten before saying his piece.

'Ianto and me've been talking about what to do for the best for you,' he told Gwilym. 'I've lived on my own since my Gwenny died and I've got used to solitary ways. I go about collecting my herbs and brewing up my potions. Sometimes people ask for my advice and I help them if I can . . .'

'You helped me, Fred,' said Ianto. 'You didn't turn away from me when my face was burned. That concoction you put on my wounds took away some of the pain and helped in the healing.'

'Yes, yes,' said Fred. 'I help people in that way, but I'm a man who likes his own company best. That's what I want to make plain.'

Fred doesn't want me under his roof, thought Gwilym. His stomach tightened with familiar dread.

'Don't take this to heart,' advised Fred, seeing Gwilym's expression. 'You're a good enough lad. Find a nice family who'll take you in.'

'What family would want me when I've not enough money to pay them for lodging?' asked Gwilym.

After more discussion Fred agreed to let Gwilym stay on in the cottage until he had earned enough money to buy lodgings elsewhere. What job could he have? Would Charlie Evans have work for him? The farrier had not promised him a job. Not really.

In any case more Tuesdays had passed than he could count, what with training for the fight. Charlie Evans would think he was unreliable, not turning up on the right Tuesday.

'I might be able to help you with a job,' said Ianto.

So Gwilym agreed to work with Ianto on the Patches. Ianto had no wish to encounter My Lady Furnace and her kisses again, so he dug ironstone from outcrops on the hillsides called the Patches. He worked the ground, but he did not own it. The land was owned by Ironmasters who paid miners for the iron ore that they found.

Ianto called for Gwilym the next morning to take him to work. Gwilym was delighted to discover that he was at last going to work with horses. One horse, anyway.

Her name was Molly, an old and patient brown mare, who pulled the wagon loaded with ironstone to the charging house. There the iron ore was tipped down the charging hole, along with lumps of limestone.

'Why limestone?' asked Gwilym.

'Helps get rid of impurities in the ironstone,' Ianto explained. 'It all goes into the fiery furnace. Takes hard work to keep My Lady Furnace fed. Hungry belly she's got.'

First they dug out the ironstone. Then they had to rid the ore of clinging earth. They laboured to heap stones and clods of earth into a dam to stop a nearby stream running downhill. The ironstone was then stacked downstream. When Ianto considered the pile was big enough to yield a fair amount of ore, he breached the dam. This was the part of the job that Gwilym learned to enjoy. The pent-up water rushed down, scouring the ironstone free of earth. They used rakes to help the process. Only then was the ore loaded into Molly's wagon.

All around them other children and adults worked at their own patches of ground. It was muddy work. Gwilym did not relish the idea of working in the rain, but that first day the sun shone and Gwilym felt cheerful enough as he worked to earn his keep. He would be on Ianto's pay roll, earning a boy's share.

Ianto tried to answer all his many questions.

'What do they do with the pig iron?'

'Refine it,' said Ianto. 'It goes into another furnace. The reverberatory furnace it's called. Tall as two men high and as long as three tall men lying end to end. Coal fires at one end separated from the pig iron in the next chamber.'

Gwilym struggled to picture what Ianto was saying. 'If the coal fire is at one end and the pig iron is in the other place how does the coal melt the iron?'

'The furnace has an arched top and the heat of the coal fire flames is turned back off the arch and down onto the pig iron,' said Ianto, wiping his hands over his face as if in remembrance of the blistering heat that had once bathed him in sweat. 'When it's all melted again a puddler stirs it up and the iron collects into lumps. I used to be a puddler,' he added with quiet pride.

Gwilym imagined a large spoon stirring the iron as if it was porridge. But wouldn't the spoon melt?

Ianto was now well into his reminiscences of his old job. 'Long iron rods, puddlers use. The furnace is all closed up but for a smallish iron door on its side. We worked in pairs. Open the door, in with the rod, stir and stir. Only a couple of minutes at a time, that was all a body could take of the heat. Blistering, it was. The mixture got heavier and heavier to handle and then the iron would collect into huge lumps. We used paddles to form the lumps into balls, and tongs to put the balls into the bogey to be rushed to be hammered and rolled into bar iron. In an eight hour shift we could do five to eight melts.'

'Why go to all that trouble when you had pig iron already?' asked Gwilym.

'Because pig iron was brittle and broke too easily. What the puddling did was improve the quality, turned the iron into wrought iron. A man called Henry Cort from Hampshire invented the process and Ironmaster Crawshay here in Iron Town was the first to use it. Peter Onions had his own idea how to improve the iron. He was from Iron Town too.'

'What do they make with all the iron?' asked Gwilym, leaning on his spade and using his question as an excuse to rest.

'Cauldrons, kettles, flat irons, hoops for wagon wheels . . .'

'Horse shoes!' chipped in Gwilym, remembering the blacksmith in Market Town.

'Yes, and anchor chains for ships, cannon balls and guns, munitions they're called.'

'Cannon balls and guns!'

'There's big battles going on; war, with soldiers and such.'

'Where?' cried Gwilym, looking around.

'Over the sea, on the Continong. We're fighting the French. They're led by a General called Boneypart. Napoleon Boneypart.'

'Why are we fighting the French?' asked Gwilym.

'Don't know. But our Admiral Nelson is glad of a means to fight them. Called in two years ago, unexpected, to Iron Town, to see where the cannon balls for his fleet are made. Famous he is, and only little, but brave. His fleet beat Boneypart in the Battle of the Nile. I saw him myself.'

'In the battle?'

'No! Iron man, I've always been; not a soldier or a sailor,' Ianto sat back on his heels, ready to tell about the famous Admiral's visit.

'Ironmaster Crawshay was all dressed up to meet Nelson. Three-quarter coat, red collar, two rows of buttons, white cravat. So excited, he called all the workmen together and yelled, "Here's Nelson! Shout, you beggars!" We all cheered. Stayed at the Star, Nelson did.'

'I'd like to see someone famous,' said Gwilym wistfully.

As they led Molly, plodding on her last trip of the day to the charging house, Ianto announced, 'Pay day Saturday. Plenty of money in the pay clerk's office on a Saturday.'

Saturday came after Friday. Why was the word Friday chiming on a memory in Gwilym's head? Jed and those men in the coaching inn. Up to no good they were. And that was to take place on a Friday.

'Ianto! There's a robber in Iron Town!' Gwilym blurted out.

'There's many a robber in Iron Town,' said Ianto calmly. 'You've met some of 'em already.'

'No, this isn't one of a gang of boys. He's a horseman. Cruel he is to his horse. He's planning some wrongdoing on a Friday,' insisted Gwilym.

He told how he'd overheard Jed and Nathan at the White Rock Tavern, and Fat Man and Weasel Face at the coaching Inn.

'Served them ale, did you, lad?'

'Yes. Jed had shining spurs and a worn-out horse. He wanted a new one, but Fat Man said it was not his business.'

Ianto was thoughtful when he heard Gwilym describe the three men.

'The man-with-the-spurs I don't know, but there are highwaymen about and he may be one. Fat Man is a pay clerk at the Ironworks' office. Weasel Face is a pal of his. Doesn't have a job, doesn't like hard work. He's just a hanger-on.'

'Where does all the money come from? Does the Ironmaster make it?'

Ianto snorted. 'He makes it, but not in the way you mean. I've told you, his ironworks produces iron. Customers buy the iron to be made into iron goods. He pays his workers, and himself, with the profit. Sometimes there's more demand for iron, like now with a war on, and the price goes up. The money is in a bank in Garrison Town twenty miles from here. It's collected on Fridays for pay-out on Saturdays. If I was your man-with-the-spurs I'd be thinking of lying in wait for the collector before he gets back to Iron Town with his bulging bags of cash.'

'What can we do to stop the thief?' Gwilym was angry at the thought of a hard-hearted ruffian stealing his hard-earned pay before he'd had a chance even to see it.

'First things first,' said Ianto. 'We'll unload the wagon, take Molly to the stables, rub her down, feed and water her, then we'll go look for Ironmaster Crawshay. He lives near his precious ironworks. You tell him what you've told me.'

Ironmaster Crawshay. He was the man who owned one of the mightiest ironworks in Iron Town: a famous man. Gwilym was daunted at the prospect of meeting him.

29

Crawshay's house was large and imposing. Directly in front of it ran a canal with barges loaded with bar iron. Horses harnessed to the barges made their way along the towpath. The house was so near the ironworks that the Crawshay family and their servants must have suffered almost as much of the clamour of the works as did the workers themselves.

The visitors were fortunate. They did not have to ask where Mr Crawshay was, for the imposing figure of the proprietor himself was making his way towards them. He was talking in a lively fashion to the two men walking beside him.

Ianto stepped forward. 'Sir,' he said, 'we have information you need to know.'

'What? What?' The Ironmaster was impatient at the interruption. Then, looking directly at Ianto he exclaimed, 'Ianto Jenkins! How are you, man?' He shook Ianto's hand vigorously. Turning to his companions, he said, 'Mr Homfray, Mr Spenser, Ianto was one of my best men until . . .' he left the rest unsaid for Ianto's face explained it.

The uninjured side of Ianto's face smiled.

'I'm on the Patches now. This lad, Gwilym here, works with me. New to Iron Town he is. He has something important to tell you.'

Gwilym was unsure where to start his story. He tumbled out a jumble of words that did not make sense even to him, and he was supposed to know what he was talking about.

'There's this man . . . heard him talking . . . to this other man . . . money for the taking in Iron Town he said. Miles away he was . . . then I came here . . . and there he was again.'

'Who is this man?' asked Mr Crawshay, confused.

'The man-with-the-shiny-spurs. Cruel to his horse. This man; I saw him again, at the coaching inn talking to two men. Fat Man and Weasel Face . . . and they said Friday.'

Gwilym stopped. His story sounded daft. Ianto tried to help.

'Gwilym was walking to Iron Town . . .'

'To find a job,' explained Gwilym.

Ianto went on to help make sense of what tongue-tied Gwilym had been trying to say. 'He was trying to get a better horse. It wasn't the talk of an honest man, sir. He may be a cutpurse, or a highwayman; anyway a thief of some sort. When Gwilym was potboy at the coaching inn, the Crown it was probably, here in Iron Town, the man-with-the-spurs was there. He was seeking information . . .'

'And Fat Man was ready to give it,' added Gwilym.

'Information involving money no doubt,' said Mr Crawshay. 'I know the significance of Friday. That is the day that Mr Spenser here will act as courier to collect our workers' pay from Garrison Town.'

'The thief will be lying in wait, sir,' warned Ianto.

'There'll be other travellers on the road I'll be on. How is he to know who to waylay?' asked Mr Spenser.

Gwilym suddenly remembered. 'Black horse!' he blurted out. 'Black horse, white star blaze, two white legs, right foreleg, left hind leg. That's what Fat Man said.'

Mr Spenser was startled. 'My horse!' he said. 'That's a description of the horse I always ride to Garrison Town. It goes at a good, steady, gallop. That's why I always take Sureshot on Fridays.'

'There you have it, sir,' said Ianto.

Mr Crawshay's face was grim. 'You've both done me good service,' he said. 'I believe I know who the informants are. One of them is in my employ. I'll keep an eye on 'em. Don't want to alarm them yet. We'll catch 'em if they're guilty. You're a good lad, Gwilym, with sharp eyes and ears and a good brain behind 'em. If there is any truth in what you tell me it is as well to be forewarned.'

Mr Homfray, who had listened intently to the conversation, made his own comment on the situation. 'Perhaps the villain has heard of our wager, Crawshay,' he suggested. 'Such a man would be interested in our thousand-guinea wager on my experiment with Mr Trevithick's invention, think you?' He smiled as if at a private joke.

'Have you heard of our wager, Ianto?' asked Mr Crawshay. 'It is no mere rumour.'

'How did it come about?' asked Ianto.

'As you can see, the canal here carries my iron straight from my works, down the valley to Seaport Town. From there it goes by ship to where my customers can buy it. This gives me an unfair advantage, so say my rivals in the trade – Mr Homfray here is one – who have their works on the eastern side of the valley.'

Mr Homfray replied, 'So we easterners, as you might call us on the other side of the valley, put our hands in our pockets and paid for a tramroad on which to haul our iron down the nine miles to the canal basin where we too can take advantage of the canal to Seaport Town.'

'But my barges,' went on Mr Crawshay, 'riding easy on the water, drawn by one horse, can ship out tons more iron than their horse-drawn trams on rails.'

'We'll be on more even terms when Mr Trevithick finishes his new invention,' said Mr Homfray confidently.

'A steam locomotive moving on rails will never work, Homfray. I've said so before and backed my judgement with 500 guineas.'

'And I've wagered my 500 guineas that the clever Cornishman will succeed,' Mr Homfray responded. 'This thief we are hearing about may well think that a bag of gold will be handed over when I win the wager.'

'You may be right,' said Mr Crawshay, 'but the men's pay will be the easier to try for. Keep me informed of any developments,' he told the two friends. Then with an abrupt 'good day', the ironmaster and his two companions strode away.

'Who is Mr Homfray?' asked Gwilym.

'He is a rival ironmaster, as he said,' replied Ianto.

'They seem friendly enough,' said Gwilym, falling into step as they made their way back from the Ironmaster's house.

'Friendly as man to man, rivals in the iron trade. There's been dispute between them ever since the canal opened in 1795, nine years ago. It's true Mr Crawshay has the advantage of the new canal right on the doorstep of his ironworks.'

'A thousand guineas was the wager between them. I didn't know there was that much money to be had by working for it, let alone a bet between two men,' said Gwilym.

'Five hundred each,' corrected Ianto.

'One thousand or five hundred, it's a lot of money. I wonder what such a lot of money looks like.'

'I don't know, lad. There's some mystery about the new invention that Mr Homfray says will win him his wager.'

'Why a mystery?'

'No-one but the inventor, two mechanics and Mr

Homfray himself really know what it can do. It's in a workshed at Mr Homfray's ironworks,' said Ianto.

'I'd like to see it,' said Gwilym.

'It'll be there for all to see on the twenty-first of this month. That's the day they say has been chosen to test the invention and win or lose the wager.'

In silence they walked across the workyard. Gwilym sensed Ianto's sadness.

'What's the matter?' he asked, touching his friend's arm.

'Crawshay remembered me. One of his best men, he said I was. Now look at me. Scratching away on the Patches.'

'Without scratching away on the Patches there'd be no ironstone for the furnaces. You're still an ironman, Ianto,' said Gwilym.

Ianto looked fully at the boy. 'You give a man back a bit of self-respect. You're a good 'un,' he said.

Gwilym had never received such praise. First from the Ironmaster himself and now from his friend. He suddenly clutched Ianto's sleeve. Two men had appeared in the doorway of an office building, one of the many buildings skirting the yard.

'It's them. Over there,' he whispered.

Ianto glanced in their direction, not making too much of his interest. One man was corpulent, his waistcoat straining at its buttons. The other man carried a sheaf of papers in his bony hands; his legs were thin, his nose long. The fat man took a jingling bunch of keys from his pocket and turned to close and lock the door.

Gwilym slid to hide behind Ianto, fearful that the men might recognise him. Ianto watched grimly as the men left the yard.

'It has to be those two you saw at the Crown. That's the pay office they've locked up. They'd know to a farthing how much money comes from Garrison Town's bank for pay day. The villains. Knowing how hard we all work for an honest wage and they sneak their knowledge to a grubby, grabbing thief!'

'Who's cruel to his horse,' said Gwilym adding to Jed's iniquities.

'. . . sharing the spoils with him, no doubt,' Ianto went on.

Dusk was falling and Iron Town's surrounding slag heaps, subdued by the brightness of day, once more glowed dully scarlet under the darkening sky.

There was light enough to see to walk safely. Talking quietly as they walked, they did not at first spy, some distance ahead, the figure of a limping man.

Seeing Ianto and Gwilym, he shouted, stumbled, almost fell in his effort to run towards them.

30

The limping man's dark blue coat was torn, his breeches muddied; blood dripped from a wound on the side of his head, staining his white linen shirt.

'Robbed!' he cried. 'I've just been robbed, money taken, my fine horse stolen from me and a pistol fired at me in fighting my attacker.'

'I know you!' exclaimed Gwilym. 'I held your horse for you at the Crown!'

The man looked at him with no sign of knowing him, then caught sight of Ianto's full face. His shocked look prompted a reassuring response.

'I'm no devil, though I may look like one,' Ianto said gently.

'Ironman, are you?' asked the man with understanding.

'Aye,' replied Ianto. 'This lad here may have seen the man who had need of a fine horse and no honest money to pay for it. Gwilym is the lad's name. I'm Ianto Jenkins, and you, sir, need help.'

Where would they go but to the one man they knew who was skilled in the art of healing? Frederick the Great opened his cottage door, saw the state of the stranger's head and opened the door wider to admit his visitors.

The limping man's name was Henry Dobbs. He was in town to buy bar iron for his father's manufactory, and to check on its quality. This he told them while Fred cleaned and bandaged his head wound.

'The thief came at me out of the shadows,' he said. 'He pointed a pistol at me. Demanded money. I was dragged off my horse. That's when I sprained my ankle. He jumped into the saddle. I caught hold of the stirrup to stop him getting away; he lashed out with his spurred boot, kicked me in the head. The blow sent me flying into the ditch. He galloped off, leaving his own sorry mare behind. Her sides were raked raw. Poor creature, quite frantic at the commotion we'd made, loose reins flapping and stirrups whipping her, she raced past me too fast for me to catch her.'

'Jed,' said Gwilym. 'It had to be Jed who robbed you.'

Gwilym and Ianto told Fred and Henry Dobbs the tale of Gwilym's encounters with the robber, as Fred calmly went on to bandage Mr Dobbs's sprained ankle.

'We fear he is planning to rob the courier who brings the ironworkers' pay from Garrison Town,' said Ianto.

'The villain!' exclaimed Henry Dobbs. 'We must stop him. We must tell Ironmaster Crawshay.'

'He knows,' said Ianto.

'What is he going to do? We must find out. We must help catch the thief,' said Henry Dobbs.

Very ready with his 'we must help', thought Gwilym. It would be nice to be asked first if 'we' were inclined to risk in the helping.

Worked up into a state of fury by his sufferings and the tale he had heard, Mr Dobbs insisted on being taken immediately to see the Ironmaster.

Mr Crawshay, inviting them into his wide hallway with surprised cordiality, was most solicitous of Mr Dobbs's welfare. He was after all a potential customer and one whom Mr Homfray too would be pleased to meet.

After much anxious discussion it was agreed that an attempt should be made to intercept the thief. Together they discussed how best to do it. Would volunteers come forward, knowing that Jed now had a fast horse, a pistol, and a ruthless will to use it?

31

'I'll see to the volunteers,' said Mr Crawshay. How much choice would men have if the Ironmaster himself was asking for their help, Gwilym thought. Still, it was their own pay they would be protecting.

'I'd like to be the first to volunteer, sir,' said Ianto resolutely.

Mr Crawshay nodded approvingly.

'Good man,' he said.

'Naturally I wish to play my part in apprehending the rascal,' said Henry Dobbs.

'Certainly,' said Mr Crawshay.

'I'm a volunteer too,' piped up Gwilym.

The men laughed. Gwilym scowled. He felt a proprietory interest in Jed.

'You've done your job already, lad, warning us about Jed and what he was up to. He's got a gun and he's dangerous. You stay safe at home,' said Mr Crawshay.

Gwilym was not pleased by this order.

He was to miss all the fun, was he? Not if he could help it.

In the dark early hours of the Friday morning, when hoar frost sparkled in the cold moonlight, the volunteers gathered at the Ironmaster's house finally to plan what they were to do. Slipping after them, a shadow among shadows, was Gwilym. Fred had made no sound in his curtained bed, and Gwilym had taken care not to make a noise as he opened the door to leave the cottage. Fred could not stop him now.

Lamplight spilled onto the frost-silvered ground as the door opened for the men to leave the Ironmaster's house. Hastily Gwilym flattened himself back against the side wall. Cautiously, he peered from his hiding place and recognised the three men with Ianto.

They were Shenkin Jones, Dafydd Evans and Will the Mill, tough young men, work-hardened, and known to be ready with their fists. Shenkin had a cudgel held loose in his right hand.

Where was Mr Dobbs who was so ready with his 'we must help'? Why had he failed to turn up?

Shenkin was quietly repeating final instructions. 'Remember, it's Sureshot Jed will be looking out for: black, white star blaze, white right foreleg, white left hindleg. You fix that in your minds too, boys.'

'Fixed it is,' murmured Dafydd.

'He won't know who's riding, what with the cloak on and the hood up,' went on Shenkin. 'I've told you the two places Jed might lie in ambush and where we can hide near both of them. If he's not in the first place nearest Garrison Town we're to fall back to the second place, not showing ourselves but keeping pace with the black horse.'

Shenkin knew every bit of rock and rubble, every hiding place in bracken or scrub, in and around Iron Town and the turnpike road to Garrison Town. He was a poacher in his spare time but no-one let on that they knew how his knowledge was gained.

'I'd better be look-out, my eyesight's better than any of yours,' whispered Will the Mill.

'What about a warning signal when Sureshot comes into sight?' was Ianto's quiet question.

'I'll mew like a buzzard,' said Will.

'It'll be daylight. There's lots of buzzards flying around in daylight. Confusing.'

'I'll hoot like an owl then,' said Will.

'That'll do,' said Ianto.

Silently they moved into the darkness, unaware that they were being followed.

32

There was only one turnpike road leading from Garrison Town into Iron Town. It crossed a bleak mountain range then entered a valley with rocky outcrops rising high on one side, and with woods of oak, ash and sycamore trees on the other. Hawthorn, blackthorn and winter-brown bracken thickly bordered much of the road as it wound its way to the toll house at Iron Town.

Gwilym kept close behind the ambush men for five miles, but finally could not keep up with them. Angry with himself for lagging behind, he stopped to gain breath, and wait for the pain from the stitch in his side to ease. Not risking to be seen, he crouched down in the bracken.

Daybreak came, revealing a light mist in the valley.

Gwilym shivered, only partly from the cold. Listening for the hoot of an owl and the clatter of hoofbeats, his ears strained to catch distant sounds. Instead he heard bracken rustle nearby and the stamp of hooves on soft ground.

Cautiously he raised his head above the bracken.

Jed!

Only a tall man's length away! It was Jed, astride Henry Dobbs's stolen horse, grim-faced, pistol in hand, staring!

Mercifully, he was gazing unblinkingly in the direction of the road. Low hung branches of an old oak tree concealed him.

Gwilym silently lowered himself back into his hiding place. His heart thumped loud as the hammers in the ironworks. Could Jed hear it? His mouth was dry.

What had gone wrong?

Somehow Jed had unknowingly foiled the men at the ambush points.

He could not warn the men without alerting Jed. He would have to do something himself. The wavering call of an owl interrupted his racing thoughts. It was the signal that Mr Spenser, the courier with the men's wages, was in sight. What could he do?

The steady beat of hooves echoed back from the rocks. Rounding a bend in the turnpike road cantered the black horse with a white star blaze and two white legs, right foreleg, left hindleg.

Clack! Jed's pistol was ready to fire. Gwilym risked another look.

The highwayman, reins gathered tightly in his left hand, pistol in his right, jabbed his shining spurs into his stolen mount's flanks to urge it forward.

33

A loud scream rang out. It startled Jed's horse and warned the courier. It startled Gwilym too. He didn't know he could make such a racket!

Seeing the highwayman move to attack had been too much for Gwilym's sense of justice. He rushed out of his hiding place, crashed through the bracken, yelling at the top of his voice.

Jed fought to control his plunging, spinning mount. Gwilym stopped dead, keeping clear of flashing hooves. Jed glared at him. Gwilym had never seen such a coldly hostile stare: not even Jethro's had been so frightening.

There was no excitement now, only terror. If he'd had sense he would have sunk back into the cover of the bracken. But his senses had left him. With his feet welded to the ground, he waited for the pistol shot that would surely come.

Not for the first time in his life, Gwilym felt completely alone. A low angry growl came from Jed's throat.

'You interfering guttersnipe, you don't know what you've done!' he shouted hoarsely.

'Oh yes, he does,' said a familiar voice.

It was Ianto. He and his companions rose from the bracken and surrounded Jed. Shenkin knocked the pistol from Jed's grasp with a swift tap of his cudgel. Dafydd grasped the reins and quietened the horse. Will grasped Jed, dragged him from the saddle and Ianto tied the highwayman's hands. Shenkin stood ready to administer another tap with his cudgel if Jed showed any signs of fight. But without his pistol he was no fighter.

'Well done, men!'

Henry Dobbs rode up, the hood of his riding cloak pushed back, beaming with delight. His stolen horse snickered a response to a voice it knew.

'How did you know?' growled Jed.

'Don't tell him,' ordered Ianto.

'You had something to do with it. I can feel it in my bones,' Jed glowered at Gwilym.

'If you had attacked me you'd have gained only these,' said Henry Dobbs.

He flipped open the saddle bags. They were full of worthless stones, as Gwilym's pouch had been.

Henry Dobbs dismounted from Sureshshot's back and examined the mare Jed had stolen from him. Her flanks, too, showed the cruel marks left by his spurs.

Gwilym was glad to see him. He had been disappointed that Mr Dobbs had failed to join the ambush party, especially as he had shown such a desire to catch the thief. Now he realised that his role had been to play the decoy courier.

Where was Mr Spenser, the real courier? The real money for the ironworkers' wages? Ironmaster Crawshay had said he might have a riot on his hands if the workers did not get their pay.

It was a jubilant little procession that made its way to Iron Town. Jed, hands tied behind his back, trudged the road, guarded by the ambush men. Henry Dobbs rode his own mare. Gwilym, triumphant, sat high up in the saddle of Sureshot as a reward for his part in Jed's capture.

Holding the reins, riding like a rich man, he suddenly recalled the last ride he had had, saddleless, breathless, on the back of an impudent mountain pony.

34

The procession made its way into town, gathering a crowd of followers as it went. Bobbing up and down, trying to get a glimpse of what was causing all the excitement, were Billy Big Hat, Guto and the gang. Gwilym, from his lofty perch atop Sureshot, waved a lordly hand at them.

'Think you've gone up in the world, country bumpkin!' shouted Billy. 'Mind you don't come a cropper!'

Gwilym grinned. 'You're jealous!' he shouted back.

They went to Ironmaster Crawshay's house. A great welcome and the Parish Constable himself awaited them. The whole household seemed to be crammed into the hallway. When Henry Dobbs explained Gwilym's part in the capture there was such a fuss made of the boy that the Constable regretted he had not taken part himself.

'Well done, lad!' cried Mr Crawshay. 'Now the Constable can lock the villain up.'

Jed was led away, his dark eyebrows drawn together in a ferocious scowl. As he passed Gwilym he said, with soft-spoken menace, 'I won't forget what you've done, boy.'

Gwilym turned to Mr Crawshay. 'Sir,' he said, 'how will the workers be paid? There were only stones in Mr Dobbs's saddlebags.'

'Well, Gwilym, we had two plans, d'yer see. One was to ambush the thief. The other was to bring the wages safely over the mountain by a little-known track.

'That's what we were doing!'

Gwilym turned. Newly arrived, mud-spattered from a long and difficult ride, came Mr Spenser, saddlebags slung over his shoulder, accompanied by Frederick the Great.

'You were asleep in your bed when I left this morning,' Gwilym said to Fred.

'Whatever time you left, I left before you,' explained Fred. 'Mr Spenser needed a guide over the mountain and a strong man to guard him and the money, should there be any other trouble. We had the loan of horses from Mr Crawshay's stable.'

Mr Spenser thankfully dropped the heavy saddlebags to the floor. Gwilym hoped he would open them so he could see the money they had all risked their lives for, but the Ironmaster said, 'Bring the bags into my office for safe keeping.'

Only the courier and Mr Crawshay entered the office, shutting the door behind them. Then, through the stout wood of the door, Gwilym heard the dull clang of iron.

'What was that?' he asked Ianto.

'That was the sound of the safe door slamming closed,' Ianto said, and explained what a safe was.

So that's another thing iron is made into, thought Gwilym.

'Now, what all you good men need is a hearty breakfast inside you,' suggested the hospitable Mr Crawshay when he rejoined them. 'Into the kitchen with you. Mrs Katie Lewis will look after you. Spenser and I have our work to do now.'

All the household servants returned to their duties. From the kitchen came an appetising smell of frying bacon. Dafydd, Shenkin, Will the Mill, Ianto, Frederick the Great and Gwilym followed the scent like hungry foxes. Mrs Lewis, a plump and smiling woman with a large white apron over her brown dress, greeted them warmly.

'Sit you down, gentlemen,' she invited. 'Eat your fill.'

With much scraping of chair-legs on the stone floor, the ambush men, Fred and Gwilym, sat at the table. Dafydd's belly rumbled loudly and everyone laughed. Gwilym had never seen so much food.

Steaming bowls of porridge were first set before them on the scrubbed-top wooden table. Ianto passed the salt for Gwilym to add savour to the oatmeal. Soon emptied, the bowls and spoons were cleared away by the kitchen maids.

Plates, forks and knives were put before the guests and then huge pewter platters covered in sizzling slices of bacon were brought, from which they were urged to help themselves.

Seated at the head of the table, Mrs Lewis cut away at a large loaf of bread, trying to keep up with requests for more to dip into the delicious juices that came from the meat.

Even after he was full, Gwilym asked for more bread, slipping it into his pockets when he thought no-one was looking.

Mrs Lewis noticed. She kept back a spare slice of bacon to give him when he left.

'To go with the bread in your pockets,' she said. Gwilym blushed. He was no better than Jed. He had acted like a thief.

Mrs Lewis smiled, though.

35

One day a hero, the next in trouble again. Ianto and Fred gave him a right telling off. He had put himself in danger for no reason; had no business following the ambush men. Might have ruined their chances of catching the thief.

'I don't care what you say. It's a good thing I was where I was or you wouldn't have caught him,' Gwilym responded indignantly. 'If it hadn't been for me, no-one would have known about Jed and there'd have been a riot; Mr Crawshay said so, and I wanted to see him caught.'

'All right, boy,' said Ianto more calmly. 'We didn't want you to get hurt, see. You were a brave lad to stand and face Jed and his loaded pistol. Fair play,' and he clapped a consoling hand on Gwilym's angry shoulder.

Gwilym decided not to confess that it was not bravery but fright that caused him to stand his ground against Jed's weapon. He asked, 'How did you all come along at just the right time?'

Ianto explained that when Jed did not appear at the farthest ambush point, they moved to the one nearer Iron Town. 'Henry Dobbs reined in Sureshot to an easy pace so that we could keep up with them as we went through the bracken and bushes, keeping hidden ourselves but keeping him in sight. We knew if we kept close to Henry Dobbs, Jed would strike sooner or later. The place he chose wasn't the best ambush point. Shenkin was mad he hadn't thought of that spot. Jed was a stranger to the area so he wouldn't know the best ones to hide in. Probably picked the first likely hiding place he came across.'

'What will happen to Jed now?' asked Gwilym.

'He'll be sent to the Assizes in Market Town. Maybe if he's found guilty he'll be sent to the penal colony in Australia.'

'He's guilty all right,' said Fred. 'He didn't get away with the workers' pay but tried his best, and . . .'

'. . . and he stole a horse and was cruel to that one as well,' interrupted Gwilym.

'And he kicked Henry Dobbs in the head,' added Ianto.

'He was not a nice man,' said Gwilym. His friends laughed. 'What about Fat Man and Weasel Face?' asked Gwilym.

'He means Dodgson and Williams,' said Ianto. 'Crawshay will deal with them. No doubt they'll deny any part in the plot. They'll be shocked they've been found out.'

The friends' pleasure at having averted the robbery did not last long. Someone knocked loudly on the cottage door. Fred hastened to open it. Shenkin rushed in.

'The ruffian has escaped!' he shouted.

36

The friends listened to Shenkin's tale with dismay. Not only Jed but Fat Man, the wages clerk, and Weasel Face had disappeared too. Ironmaster Crawshay had summoned them to his office to answer questions about their meeting with the highwayman. They denied any knowledge of Jed. But they had taken fright and left Iron Town in the middle of the night. How Jed had escaped was still a bit of a mystery.

'Somehow the door of the lock-up was opened. Constable Jones is furious because it was probably opened with his own key,' said Shenkin. 'Soon after he put Jed into jail, a gang of street urchins crowded around him asking for money. They didn't pester him for long. As soon as he told them to go away and stop bothering him, they went, quite docile. He reckons they'd lifted his key by then and didn't hang around in case he realised what they'd done. He didn't notice the key was missing until this morning.'

'It was Billy Big Hat's gang,' said Gwilym. 'Had to be. They must have teamed up with Jed.'

'A gang of boys like that would have useful information for him, a stranger to Iron Town, if he was willing to pay for it,' agreed Ianto.

'. . . or to share in whatever spoils resulted,' added Fred.

'Jed won't get far. He has no money, no horse,' said Shenkin.

'He'll go where there's a smell of gold,' said Ianto.

'There'll be a smell of gold here in Iron Town on Tuesday,' said Shenkin. 'It's the day the wager will be decided. Five hundred guineas apiece, that's what Samuel Homfray and Richard Crawshay are putting up.'

Anyone who thought the newfangled contraption could draw ten tons of iron without the aid of horses must be stupid, thought Gwilym. Who but rich men would think of wasting their money on such a scheme? He'd like to see it so that he could jeer at it.

'Homfray is an arrogant and overbearing man, so I've heard,' said Fred.

Shenkin, now seated comfortably with them around the fire, disagreed.

'He's good enough to his workmen and always on the look-out for new ideas to improve the works,' he said and went on to tell them what he knew.

Four years previously, Ironmaster Homfray had invited Richard Trevithick, an engineer from

Cornwall, to design and build a new forge engine for his ironworks. They got on well together. Now the Cornishman had been called in again to win the wager for Homfray.

For some time Trevithick, Rees Jones the mechanic and William Davies had been constantly in each others' company, working on the new engine. Richard Brown had made the boiler and Rees Jones did most of the fitting.

'Crawshay would dearly love to know what's going on behind the doors of Trevithick's workshop on Homfray's yard,' said Shenkin.

Gwilym, gazing sleepily into the dancing flames of the fire, had already decided that he would find out for himself.

37

After all the excitement of Jed's capture and escape, Gwilym found it hard to settle to the dreary task of helping Ianto work his Patch. The prospect of finding out what was being made in Homfray's yard was the one thing that kept his mind lively.

After the last load of the day had been hauled to the charging house, and Molly had been stabled, fed and watered, Gwilym was free to satisfy his curiosity. Ianto went off to his lodging house, thinking Gwilym would go to Fred's place.

With new-found confidence, Gwilym asked a passer-by the way to Homfray's Ironworks. The man clapped his hands over his pockets and took a quick glance behind him to check that Gwilym had no accomplice.

Gwilym grinned.

'No, I'm not in Billy Big Hat's gang,' he said.

The man grunted, still suspicious, but told him where to go.

In the gathering gloom of evening, Gwilym stepped across the tram tracks that wound across Homfray's workyard. It seemed familiar. Then Gwilym recognised it was the ironworks where he'd been half-promised a job, when he first arrived in Iron Town.

Looking around to see which of the many buildings might house the invention, he noticed that one workshop had its doors firmly shut. Loud noises, hissing, scraping and clanking came from inside. Then the doors were flung wide open.

Lit by flames, shrouded in clouds of steam, was an amazing object. Gwilym stopped in his tracks. Dragon, thought Gwilym. It's breathing fire and steam like a dragon. It drew a great shuddering breath of steam and began to move. It moved towards him! Rods of iron punched forward and backwards from the engine's sides.

'Out of the way, boy!'

The warning shout was from William Davies, bravely coming from somewhere amidst the dragon's steam and smoke. Gwilym jumped aside.

With a grinding of iron wheels on iron track the dragon crept forward into the centre of the yard. A very tall, begrimed and shirt-sleeved man strode beside it. The dragon halted, quietly panting, like a beast.

'What do you think of it, boy?' Richard Trevithick asked a dumbfounded Gwilym.

'I thought it was a fire-breathing dragon,' said Gwilym, recovering from his shock.

'You're not the first one to be frightened by my locomotives,' said Trevithick, wiping his oily hands on a rag tucked into his belt. 'One was called a puffing devil by a woman who should have known better.'

'What is it, sir?' asked Gwilym.

'It's a high pressure steam tram engine, capable of pulling ten tons of iron, and more,' said Trevithick. 'My latest invention,' he added. 'There's many a powerful steam engine driving the industrial revolution we are living through, boy. Some are as big as houses, and about as mobile. My compact little beauties are just as powerful and can move, as you've just seen. The secret is in containing the high pressure and controlling it. Mind you, some of mine have blown up.'

Gwilym took a step back. Trevithick let out a shout of laughter.

'Horses are safer,' ventured Gwilym.

'Are you daring to argue with me, boy? I have a hot temper.'

'Like a dragon?' risked Gwilym.

'I have been known to up-end a man whose views I did not agree with,' warned Trevithick. 'I not only up-ended him, I planted his footprints on the ceiling!'

'So watch out,' said William Davies with a smile.

'My engines are safe now, for I invented a device

to prevent explosions in high pressure engines. In Cornwall, where I come from, my engines have travelled on roads. They can go backwards as well as forwards and with just as much strength.'

'Is this steam invention going to win the wager for Ironmaster Homfray, sir?' asked Gwilym.

'Steam locomotive,' corrected Trevithick. 'We hope so. It is an experiment, and I am confident my calculations are correct, but some people won't mind if I fail. Tuesday is the day. Wish us good fortune. There's a thousand guineas and my reputation riding on the dragon's back on Tuesday.'

He climbed up beside William Davies. Rees Jones joined them. The three men, absorbed in checking the condition of their precious high pressure steam locomotive, took no more notice of Gwilym.

He had come to make fun of the thing, but the inventor's passion for his new ideas made Gwilym stop and think. What future would horses have in a world of high pressure steam engines that could move on rail or road?

38

Ianto and Fred did not believe him, of course.

'I've seen a dragon,' he said importantly.

'Oh yes,' said Ianto, 'what do you know about dragons?'

'My Dada told me stories. They breathe fire. I've seen the Cornishman's dragon. The one that's going to win the wager for Ironmaster Homfray.' Disappointed that his remark had not caused more of a sensation, he added, 'There's a thousand guineas riding on the dragon's back; Mr Trevithick said so.'

'I'll believe this dragon of yours only when I see it,' said Ianto.

Iron Town was agog with excitement on wager day: February 21, 1804. So on that Tuesday when the three friends walked across to Ironmaster Homfray's workyard, half of Iron Town tramped along with them, eager to see what mysterious machine had been created.

'There hasn't been a turn-out like this since Admiral Nelson came to Crawshay's ironworks,' said Fred.

The high pressure steam locomotive was already out of its shed, polished and gleaming.

'Call that a dragon!' jeered Ianto.

Seen in the bright light of day the locomotive was smaller than Gwilym had imagined. Sturdy and workmanlike, its cylinder-shaped body was a boiler containing the water needed to make steam. Within was the firebox to heat the water. A hundredweight of coal to feed the fire was stacked in a tram. One large wheel and two smaller wheels were on one side of the boiler. On the other side was a complicated arrangement of wheels, with square teeth all around them, that looked as though they were going to grind into each other. Gwilym could not make head nor tail of it. There were teeth protruding from two wheels on the track as well. A chimney stack rose high above, iron rods were at the sides, more rods stuck out in front of the boiler, opposite the stack. Already the machine was shackled to the trams that were to test its power.

Three ironmasters were present: Richard Crawshay, looking confident; Samuel Homfray, looking cheerful; Richard Hill, anxious, for Mr Hill had the task of seeing the conditions of the wager were kept.

Trevithick the engineer, Rees Jones the mechanic and William Davies, who had the honour of being the locomotive driver, were talking together. The driver climbed up onto the platform of wooden boards that surrounded the engine and stoked the fire.

The firebox blazed, the steam pressure rose. So did the excitement in the crowd. Chained together behind the locomotive were a number of trams already loaded with the agreed amount of ten tons of bar iron. The rival ironmasters, Mr Hill and their officials were in another. The rest of the trams were empty, but not for long.

Trevithick urged men in the crowd, 'Jump up! Jump up!'

Seventy of them eagerly accepted the invitation.

'Their weight should add five more tons to the load!' said Trevithick.

How could he dare to be so confident?

Gwilym felt a surge of affection and anxiety for the engine. Would it pass this terrible test of strength? As Trevithick prepared to join William Davies and Rees Jones on the engine's platform, he noticed Gwilym at the front of the crowd.

'You too, Dragon Boy. There's room for a little 'un up here!'

Gwilym scrambled aboard, aided by the inventor, leaving behind his two surprised companions.

William Davies made his final checks. Smoke streamed from the stack, the rods moved slowly and with a grinding shudder the toothed wheels locked together to set themselves in motion; in obedience the wheels on the track turned. The Dragon was on its way, bravely hauling its immense burden behind it.

The crowd cheered. In the middle of them all were Ianto and Fred, waving to Gwilym. He gave a cheerful wave back to them. Why weren't they looking happier? He was safe enough in Trevithick's care.

Ianto was yelling something. Gwilym couldn't catch all the words. 'Behind you! . . . Watch out!'

39

Watch out for what? Gwilym didn't care. He was riding the dragon. The breeze ruffled his hair, wafted sooty specks and the smell of hot oil and metal. Gwilym's left eye started to stream with tears as smut from the smoke stack lodged under his eyelid.

Richard Trevithick handed him a handkerchief as the tears flooded the speck away.

'It's going nice and steady, sir,' shouted Gwilym, wiping his eyes.

'Five miles an hour, boy!' shouted the inventor.

Through Iron Town they rolled. Bystanders waved their hats and cheered. Some townsfolk just stared at the sight of a steam engine that moved.

Its iron wheels gripped tramroad rails that had only known the weight of a load that horses could pull. Gwilym leaned over the side to see the fascinating sight of the toothed wheels meshing into each other. He glanced ahead – and saw danger!

'SIR! SIR!' he cried out, tugging Trevithick's sleeve. 'The tunnel!'

The dark maw of the tramroad tunnel gaped in front of them.

High enough for a man and horse to go through, it was too low for the locomotive's chimney stack.

There was going to be a crash.

How could anyone stop this engine?

With a horse you could shout Whoa! and pull on reins.

Trevithick had the answer.

'Reverse the engine, William!'

The rods and wheels shuddered into reverse action. Sparks flew and the engine squealed to a halt. The top of the stack hit the portal and dislodged a stone.

The trailing trams crashed into one another, knocking passengers off balance. Mr Crawshay's hat tilted over his eyes, Mr Homfray staggered and Mr Hill fell against the side and bruised himself, putting him in a bad mood.

Trevithick and Rees Jones jumped down to examine the problem. The chimney stack was dented but the two men seemed not to be perturbed. The dislodged stone was shifted.

'We'll lower the stack as we go through,' said the inventor.

Rees Jones nodded. 'It's a good thing we built in the hinges for just such a possibility,' he said.

'There's another problem,' called William Davies. 'The tram rails aren't centred. They'll have to be shifted to the middle to give headroom for the flywheel to get through the tunnel.'

It was true. Fortunately the track took a central path further in. Advice and offers of help came from the passengers.

One voice of authority rose above the hubbub.

'No help, no help! The wager is off if help is accepted!' It was the voice of Mr Hill.

William and Rees looked surprised and angry.

'No arguing. I'll do it,' Trevithick told them quietly. He strode into the tunnel and began lifting and re-laying the rail plates. Gamely he laboured alone. It took some time.

Gwilym thought it was most unfair of Mr Hill. Who had made these conditions? At last Trevithick finished the extra task he had been unexpectedly set, and climbed back on to the platform.

'Well done,' said Rees Jones. William Davies gave a sympathetic nod of agreement and set about getting steam up again. Slowly the pressure rose and the locomotive moved into the darkness of the tunnel. Flames from the firebox cast devilish shadows on its dripping stones. A dank chill ran through

Gwilym's body. In the dark he remembered the shouted cry, '. . . Watch out! Behind you!'

Who or what was behind him? Only a crowd of excited men wanting a ride on the first steam engine to travel on rails, only a crowd of excited men wanting to see a wager won – or lost. One thousand guineas' worth of excitement.

Who else would be anxious to set sight on one thousand guineas? Who else? A desperate man, penniless, and on the run from the law. A desperate and ruthless man.

In the dark confines of the tunnel, the noise of the iron wheels grinding on the flanged iron rails was flung back from the stone walls onto Gwilym's deafened ears. Smoke streamed around, choking the passengers. He could hear them coughing and spluttering. It was a relief to see brightness at the end of the tunnel.

The engine proudly emerged into daylight to be cheered by onlookers who laughed with delight to see the smoke-smudged faces of the men in the trailing trams.

Gwilym twisted around to see why they were being laughed at. He saw men laughing at each others' blackened faces.

One was angrily scrubbing his face with an already dirty handkerchief. Gwilym hooted with glee. The man removed the cloth from his face. Gwilym's mouth stayed open in astonishment.

It was Jed.

40

Gwilym turned back quickly. Perhaps Jed had not noticed him. Heart pounding, Gwilym realised there was nothing he could do until they reached the Canal Basin. It was too long a tale to explain to Mr Trevithick. In any case, he could not shout above the noise of the engine without alerting Jed himself.

The engine now rattled happily on its nine mile journey to reach the barges at the Canal Basin, a place called Navigation. Its long and heavy load was carried with ease.

Trevithick said with satisfaction, 'I doubt not but we could draw forty tons at a time, so ten tons stands no chance with it at all.'

Pale sunlight filtered through leafless trees whose branches arched above the track. It flickered over the stones to which the iron rails were fixed.

'Slow down and stop, William,' cried Trevithick. 'There's branches ahead too low for my liking.'

While he climbed down and set about clearing the way, some passengers stepped down from the trams to stretch their legs. No-one offered help for fear of breaking the conditions of the bet on which Mr Hill set such store.

Gwilym risked a quick look back when everyone returned to their places, but did not see Jed. Had he jumped down and made off into the woods? The thief had taken a risk in coming on this journey, as Crawshay would recognise him. Perhaps he'd kept the handkerchief to his face in case the ironmaster turned around and saw him.

The other passengers were still grimy from their trip through the tunnel. They were standing crammed together like sheep in a pen. Black sheep now, with their smudged faces.

Sun shone on the passing places where horses and drivers waited on their journey back up to Iron Town with their empty trams. They had given way for the wager engine to take the main track.

Gwilym waved to them as he swayed with the rhythm of the puffing new invention, remembering the horse and cart that had brought him into Iron Town. Ten tons of bar iron, seventy men and its own weight. How many work horses would be needed to shift the same load? All in one go, mind. This new iron horse would take some beating.

'We're riding an iron horse, Mr Trevithick!' he cried out.

'So my invention is no longer a dragon then?' the inventor replied with a grin.

As they steamed into sight of the Canal Basin, a waiting crowd raised a cheer. William Davies released the pressure and the locomotive, panting, sighed to a halt. Clanking and clattering, the trams banged into each other. Jerked off-balance by the jolt, passengers clutched the sides of the trams as their hats tipped over their eyes. The crowd was delighted by the comic spectacle. Gwilym jumped down to join in the fun.

Mr Homfray, beaming; Mr Crawshay a mite subdued, and Mr Hill looking important, climbed down from their transport to be greeted by the officials of the Canal Basin. Huge empty barges bobbed gently on the water of the canal, waiting delivery of their iron cargo.

The three ironmasters shook hands with each other and with Trevithick; with the driver and the mechanic; with the welcoming committee, and with each other again.

'The wager! The wager! What about the wager?' someone cried out, impatient at all the fussing.

'Forward, Mr Hill, hand me the wager money!' commanded Mr Crawshay.

Ironmaster Hill stepped forward, delved into the capacious pocket of his wide-skirted coat, and held up a large, bulging, drawstring bag.

'It's like my purse,' thought Gwilym. He was in the front of the crowd, wanting to warn the ironmasters of Jed's appearance, and disappearance from the trams, but not wanting to interrupt the ceremony.

Speaking loudly so everyone could hear, Mr Crawshay turned to Mr Homfray and, holding the bag dangling at arm's length, said, 'Sir, here is my part of the wager between us. I shall not hand it over . . .' Cries of 'Shame!' came from the crowd. Unperturbed, Mr Crawshay continued even louder, '. . . until we have made the return journey.'

'Hand it over to me then!' shouted a rough voice. A man standing unnoticed beside Gwilym reached out and grabbed the bag. Thrusting it into his pocket, the thief swiftly seized Gwilym by the collar and held a sharp knife to the boy's throat.

Jed! It was Jed, intent on revenge.

'Don't stop me or I'll slit this young villain's gizzard!' he shouted.

He had acted so quickly, people did not know what to do. Holding Gwilym in front, he forced the crowd to part. Men and women moved back, angry but unable to help for fear of risking Gwilym's life.

Jed rushed a choking Gwilym into a narrow and deserted lane. Gwilym realised the whole town was gathered at the Canal Basin. There was no help for him here.

'Thought I hadn't seen you, didn't you?' Jed mocked. 'I said I wouldn't forget you, you young jackanapes, interfering in my plans, ruining my chances.'

'You can't get far. You haven't got a horse,' said Gwilym hoarsely. His collar was still held chokingly tight.

'You're in for a surprise,' said Jed, shoving him roughly forward.

A large bay horse was being ridden up the lane towards them. In the saddle was Billy Big Hat.

41

Billy slid from the saddle.

'Tie his hands,' Jed ordered Billy. Gwilym glared. Thin rope bit into his wrists as Billy hurriedly tied him up. He tried to wriggle his hands free but Jed growled a warning. Gwilym stopped struggling as he felt blood trickle warmly down his neck. Jed's knife was as keen as landlord Llew's had been.

'One more move, one deeper cut, and you'll bleed to death,' came Jed's menacing whisper close to Gwilym's right ear.

'Get my gun,' Jed ordered Billy again.

The gun? Shenkin had knocked it out of Jed's hand. How had he got it back?

Billy drew the gun from the saddlebag.

'Point it at his belly,' said Jed.

Billy held the gun, pointing it steadily at Gwilym's middle. His bright eyes mocked Gwilym's helplessness.

Jed let go of his collar, leapt into the saddle, rattled the coin-filled bag in his pocket, spun the horse around, raked spurs along its flanks and galloped away.

'What about me!' Billy yelled after him. 'You said you'd take me with you!'

Treacherous Jed's laughter was all the response he heard. The gun in Billy's hand wavered. Jed's desertion had distracted Billy's attention. Gwilym lunged forward, struck the gun aside with his tied hands, and hit Billy's jaw with a two-handed version of a trick Frederick the Great had taught him.

Billy fell to the ground. Gwilym pounced on him.

'He promised me I could go with him if I stole a good horse . . . he promised me a share of the wager money. He promised . . .' wailed Billy.

'More fool you for believing him,' said Gwilym.

Billy, white-faced with shock and disappointment, had no fight in him. In any case, with Gwilym sitting triumphantly on his chest, he was in no good position to fight.

'How did you get the gun?'

'From the Parish Constable's lock-up when we rescued Jed. It was in a drawer in the desk.'

People had held back for fear of what Jed might do to Gwilym, but when they saw him ride off from the lane they ran to help. As he was untied, Gwilym answered a stream of questions.

Billy was seized and led off to the Navigation lock-up. Gwilym was clapped on the back so hard it made him cough.

'Good lad!'

'Brave boy!'

It was embarrassing.

He was carried back shoulder-high to where the ironmasters anxiously stood. Trevithick, the mechanic and the driver welcomed him back, glad to see him safe.

'You've been hurt, boy. The devil drew blood,' said Mr Crawshay.

'Jed got away with the money, sir,' said Gwilym, as the ironmaster drew out a large pocket handkerchief to wrap around Gwilym's wound.

'Billy Big Hat stole the horse for him to get away. He thought he was going with him. Jed rattled the money in his pocket and galloped off. I felt sorry for Billy being done like that, but not that sorry.'

'Your money bag was stolen, wasn't it?' said Mr Crawshay.

'Yes, by Billy.'

'You had to fight to get it back.'

'Yes. I had it back. Filled with stones.'

'We heard about it from Ianto. He gave us the idea.'

'What idea?'

Ironmaster Crawshay was still smiling, so were Ironmaster Homfray and Ironmaster Hill. It was Mr Crawshay's loss, for Mr Homfray did not flourish his bag of gold as Mr Crawshay had done, and Mr Hill had not ventured a penny.

'Jed got away with a purse for sure.' Mr Crawshay was quite cheerful about it. Was the man daft? 'We played a trick on him, lad,' explained the ironmaster. 'Everyone in Iron Town knew about the bet between Mr Homfray and me. So Jed would surely have heard about it. Everyone thought we would hand over the guineas in public. So Jed would have heard that too.

'A cheque drawn on the Black Ox Bank in Garrison Town is all the money Homfray and I would need to settle the wager, but for a bit of drama, a story about a bag of gold guineas was more colourful; and a temptation for a dishonest man.

'We had a private wager that Jed might try for our gold if we made a big display of handing it over.

Ianto told us about the purse you fought for, and the trick played on you. When my men learnt of Jed's attempt at stealing their pay, they struck their own coin, especially for Jed.

'That's what was in the purse Jed has just stolen,' Mr Crawshay continued. 'Iron coins. Round flat pieces of iron! Not good quality iron either!'

42

The three ironmasters laughed at Gwilym's bewildered expression.

'The thief will be rich,' said Mr Homfray, 'rich in useless pieces of iron.' So that was why they were smiling so happily. They had lost nothing of value, only a leather purse. 'Now we must get back to the business of the day,' said Mr Homfray. 'Mr Trevithick! How goes your invention? Make ready for the return journey or Mr Crawshay here will claim I've not won my wager.'

The iron bars had already been unloaded onto barges now sunk low under their weighty cargo. On the towpath, their harness traces dipping into the water, stood the patient barge horses, waiting for the order to pull away on their sixteen-mile journey to Seaport Town.

As the barge horses plodded away, their mechanical rival stood solidly on the track awaiting its next move, as patient as any horse and, as an admirer had said, just as 'tractable', just as easily managed.

Fussed over by its mechanic, driver and inventor, it was gently puffing, gathering its steam power for another great effort of strength. This time to push the wagons, now ten tons less in weight, back up the gradient to Iron Town. Gwilym felt full of admiration for the thing.

Passengers climbed back into the wagons for the return trip. The ironmasters took their places, inviting Gwilym to join them. Coal was shovelled into the firebox and, with a juddering and clanking of chains and couplings, the locomotive shoved its burden away from the Canal Basin on its return journey.

'It can push as well as pull!' exclaimed Gwilym, who had expected the engine somehow to be shackled to the front again.

'Equally strong pushing or pulling,' said Mr Homfray.

Grey clouds dimmed the sun but the spirits of the travellers were high.

Suddenly the locomotive's happy rattling was disrupted by a loud bang. Metal scraped metal and the engine came slowly and sadly to a stop, amid a rush of scalding water and steam.

Trevithick and Rees Jones jumped down to find out what had happened. As they examined the damage, curious passengers climbed out of the trams.

Face grimed with oil and soot, Trevithick eventually exclaimed, 'It's no good. One of the bolts that fastens the boiler to the axle has broken and we've lost all the water.'

Mr Homfray was glum.

'Told you so, told you it wouldn't work,' gloated Mr Crawshay.

A hurried consultation took place. It was decided to send for replacements to repair the damage and for a team of horses to drag the wagons and engine to the nearest passing place where the repairs could be made without blocking the main track.

Off went the two rival ironmasters and stakeholder Mr Hill, striding briskly beside the tramway, deep in argument over what improvements could be made. The other passengers strolled after them in straggling groups.

Gwilym stayed with the disappointed engineers.

William Davies leaned against the locomotive and wiped his hands on an oily cloth. Rees Jones took out a pipe, rammed in some tobacco and lit it with a still smouldering coke raked from the firebox. Trevithick sat on the grass making calculations in a notebook pulled from his pocket.

Gwilym watched, fascinated by the inventor's scrawled writing and swiftly-drawn diagrams. Glancing up, Trevithick saw his interest.

'Would you like to be an engineer, Gwilym?'

'Can't read, can't write, Mr Trevithick,' confessed Gwilym.

'Tell Mr Crawshay you want to learn,' advised the inventor. 'He owes you a favour.'

Help came at last. A team of horses led by Mr

Homfray's stablemaster came into sight. A familiar figure walked along with them.

'Ianto!' cried Gwilym and ran to meet him.

'Are you all right, boy? Let's see what the villain did to you. Your bandage is covered in blood!'

'I'm all right. It's not a bandage – it's Mr Crawshay's handkerchief,' said Gwilym.

It took some time to harness the horses to their humiliated iron rival. It was no fire-breathing dragon now, but it was still heavy. Would the animals' flesh, blood and bone be able to haul the metal monster that had so frightened people who had first seen it?

Planting their hooves firmly into the ground, the horses heaved the wagons and engine along the track to the passing place.

Gwilym sat astride the broad brown back of Clipper, the lead horse. The sun came out again and a light wind caused the trees to nod and bow their branches at the procession. This was the way to travel.

Nothing could beat horses, not even a Dragon tamed into being an Iron Horse.

Gwilym began to whistle.

'That's a pretty tune,' said Ianto.

'My Ma's favourite song,' said Gwilym.

He was happy.